If you thought spunky Tay[...] [...]g [...] [...] in deep man-trouble in Custer County, Montana, in *The Cowboy's Lady* (Silhouette Special Edition #626), wait until you meet her sweet, citified sister, Christy....

"Will you marry me, Christy?" Cody asked.

"Oh, y-yes," she whispered.

"I mean now."

"Now?" she repeated breathlessly.

"This afternoon."

Her heart responded with a quick, wistful beat. But it was impossible.

"It . . . may be different in Montana, but Washington state has a three-day waiting period after you apply for the license," she hedged.

A slow smile eased up the corners of his mouth. "Idaho doesn't."

Dear Reader,

Welcome to the Silhouette **Special Edition** experience! With your search for consistently satisfying reading in mind, every month the authors and editors of Silhouette **Special Edition** aim to offer you a stimulating blend of deep emotions and high romance.

The name Silhouette **Special Edition** and the distinctive arch on the cover represent a commitment—a commitment to bring you six sensitive, substantial novels each month. In the pages of a Silhouette **Special Edition**, compelling true-to-life characters face riveting emotional issues—and come out winners. All the authors in the series strive for depth, vividness and warmth in writing these stories of living and loving in today's world.

The result, we hope, is romance you can believe in. Deeply emotional, richly romantic, infinitely rewarding—that's the Silhouette **Special Edition** experience. Come share it with us—six times a month!

From all the authors and editors of Silhouette **Special Edition**,

Best wishes,

Leslie Kazanjian,
Senior Editor

DEBBIE MACOMBER
The Sheriff Takes a Wife

Silhouette Special Edition

Published by Silhouette Books New York

America's Publisher of Contemporary Romance

To Merrily Boone
Friend
Title Finder
Speller of Impossible Words
Discoverer of Great Restaurants

SILHOUETTE BOOKS
300 East 42nd St., New York, N.Y. 10017

ISBN: 0-373-09637-2

First Silhouette Books printing December 1990

Printed in the U.S.A.

Books by Debbie Macomber

Silhouette Romance

That Wintry Feeling #316
Promise Me Forever #341
Adam's Image #349
The Trouble with Caasi #379
A Friend or Two #392
Christmas Masquerade #405
Shadow Chasing #415
Yesterday's Hero #426
Laughter in the Rain #437
Jury of His Peers #449
Yesterday Once More #461
Friends—and Then Some #474
Sugar and Spice #494
No Competition #512
Love 'n' Marriage #522
Mail-Order Bride #539
*Cindy and the Prince #555
*Some Kind of Wonderful #567
*Almost Paradise #579
Any Sunday #603
Almost an Angel #629
The Way to a Man's Heart #671

*Legendary Lovers Trilogy

Silhouette Special Edition

Starlight #128
Borrowed Dreams #241
Reflections of Yesterday #284
White Lace and Promises #322
All Things Considered #392
The Playboy and the Widow #482
Navy Wife #494
Navy Blues #518
For All My Tomorrows #530
Denim and Diamonds #570
Fallen Angel #577
The Courtship of Carol Sommars #606
The Cowboy's Lady #626
The Sheriff Takes a Wife #637

Silhouette Books

Silhouette Christmas Stories 1986
"Let It Snow"

DEBBIE MACOMBER

hails from the state of Washington. As a busy wife and mother of four, she strives to keep her family healthy and happy. As the prolific author of dozens of bestselling romance novels, she strives to keep her readers happy with each new book she writes.

The Sheriff Takes a Wife chronicles the head-over-heels fall taken by Christy Manning, sister of Taylor Manning Palmer, the heroine of *The Cowboy's Lady*, Silhouette Special Edition #626.

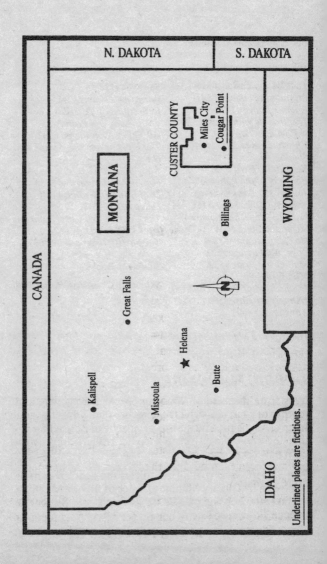

CANADA

N. DAKOTA

S. DAKOTA

MONTANA

CUSTER COUNTY

Miles City

Cougar Point

Billings

N

Great Falls

Kalispell

Missoula

Helena

Butte

WYOMING

IDAHO

Underlined places are fictitious.

Chapter One

"What do you mean you're in labor?" Christy Manning demanded of her sister.

"I didn't say that...exactly," Taylor Palmer insisted. Her palms were flattened against the protruding roundness of her abdomen. She lowered her eyelashes and released a long, slow breath.

"You can't be in labor.... I just arrived. My suitcases are still in the trunk of my car." Christy bolted to her feet and plowed the thick dark curls away from her face, using both hands. She'd been driving for nearly three days to be with her sister for the birth of this baby, but she hadn't counted on the blessed event happening quite so soon.

"What do you want me to do?" she asked, doing a masterful job collecting her poise. There was plenty of reason for alarm. The Lazy P, Russ and Taylor's cattle ranch, was miles outside of Cougar Point, the closest town. And there wasn't a neighbor in sight.

Taylor's husband, Russ, was running his sister, Mandy, over to a friend's house and doing a couple of errands before heading back to the ranch. At tops he'd be gone only an hour, or so he'd claimed.

But one hell of a lot could happen in an hour.

"I'm not convinced this is the real thing," Taylor said in an apparent effort to reassure Christy, but as she spoke her hands gently caressed her stomach. "I've never been in labor before, so I'm not sure what to expect."

In an effort to gather her scattering wits, Christy circled the kitchen table like a hungry wolf zeroing in on its prey. First and foremost, she needed to keep calm. Mentally she reviewed the recent classes she'd taken through the library. She knew CPR and enough karate to defend herself. Great. She could knock someone out and then revive him. A lot of good either of those classes was going to do her in this situation.

She swallowed a feeling of impending panic. She wasn't even supposed to be in Montana. Her mother was the one who'd planned to make the trip to be with Taylor. Only their dear, sweet mother had taken a fall and badly broken her leg. Elizabeth Manning was having trouble getting around herself and would be little or no help to Taylor. Since Christy had a couple of weeks of vacation due to her, she'd volunteered to come and be with her sister. It wasn't any great sacrifice on her part; Christy and Taylor had always been close.

Unfortunately no one had bothered to tell her she was going to be stuck alone on a cattle ranch with her nine months' pregnant sister, who just happened to be "feeling funny."

This all seemed unreal. Christy had arrived late the night before. Too late to do more than to greet everyone, haul her overnight bag into the guest bedroom and fall, exhausted, into bed.

"Stop looking like you expect to deliver this baby on your own," Taylor said, smiling up at her sister.

"But, Miss Scarlett, I don't know nothin' about birthin' no babies," Christy cried in a soft Southern drawl. She may be teasing, but what she said was the honest-to-God truth.

None of this was supposed to be happening. At least not like this. Taylor should be living in Seattle with the rest of her family. Instead, Christy's older sibling had arrived in Montana a year earlier and to everyone's surprise married a cattle rancher three months later.

At the time, Christy couldn't imagine what had possessed her cultured, cosmopolitan sister to marry someone like Russ Palmer. Especially in Reno, without a single family member present.

Their father hadn't been overly pleased to be cheated out of the chance to walk his daughter down the aisle, but once he met Russ, the rancher had won him over. Russ had reassured everyone in the family without trying. Taylor and her husband had flown into Seattle at the end of May to celebrate her parents' wedding anniversary. It was then that Taylor's husband had met Christy and her three brothers.

Taylor's eyes drifted shut a second time. The small display of pain effectively cut off Christy's thoughts. She held her breath until she saw the tension slowly ease from her sister's body. "What happened?"

"I felt a funny pain, that's all. Don't worry. It wasn't anything."

"A funny pain? And you don't want me to worry?" Christy echoed, and couldn't keep the panic from rattling her voice. "Then why do I have this incredible urge to boil water?"

Taylor, forever calm and serene in a crisis, grinned. "Don't worry. I've been having these pains off and on for the past week, only..."

"Only what?" Christy urged.

"Only these feel different. I don't know how to explain it." She rose haltingly to her feet. "I think it might be a good idea if I got dressed."

"Right," Christy said, as if the idea were a stroke of genius. "Me, too." With her arm around Taylor's thick waist, Christy led her sister down the long, narrow hallway that led to the master bedroom. "Do you need any help?"

"Don't be ridiculous!" Almost before the words had left her lips, Taylor let out a small cry and pressed her shoulder to the wall while clutching her stomach.

Christy was instantly alarmed. "What is it?"

"Oh...my." Wide-eyed, Taylor turned toward Christy. "Hurry and get some towels. My water just broke."

"Your water broke," Christy repeated in a stupor. She tossed her hands toward the ceiling as if to accuse God of this unexpected turn of events. "Her water just broke." Rushing into the bathroom, she returned with enough towels to soak up a flood.

Taylor continued to lean against the wall, breathing deeply, her eyes closed. Christy dropped the towels onto the floor, far more concerned about Taylor than a little water. "Are you all right?"

Her sister answered with a nod that said otherwise.

"I'm calling the doctor," Christy insisted. "Don't you dare move. Understand?" The sense of panic was stronger than ever, but Christy managed to swallow it. Taylor needed her; there wasn't time to be concerned with her own fears.

Taylor's doctor was in Miles City, sixty miles distant, and Christy soon learned the hospital was there. As well as she could figure, they were an hour, if not more, away. Christy spoke to Dr. Donovan briefly, and when she explained what had happened, the doctor suggested it would be a good idea if Taylor came to the hospital right away.

"I'm not going without Russ," Taylor stated adamantly when Christy relayed her conversation. "Russ will be back any minute."

Christy started to balk. It wasn't her fault that Taylor's husband had such a bad sense of timing.

"You don't know Russ the way I do," Taylor said, even before Christy had a chance to reason with her. "If he came home and found us gone—"

"I'll leave him a note. He'll understand. Then as soon as he's back, he can join us."

"No."

Christy had heard that tone of voice often enough to know there wasn't anything she could say or do that would budge that stubborn streak of Taylor's. "We can't just sit here and wait," Christy wailed.

"Of course we can. Now relax!"

"Me, relax? You're the one having the baby."

"I'm fine. Baby Palmer and mother are both calm and prepared."

Baby Palmer, Christy's mind echoed. Her only sister was about to become a mother. This wasn't new information, but the realization tugged strong chords within

Christy. Until this moment Taylor's pregnancy had seemed abstract. But here they were alone together, and suddenly this baby was very real. This tiny life was depending on Christy, and the thought was terrifying. Yet nothing she said would convince Taylor to leave for the hospital without Russ.

The next thirty minutes felt like thirty years. Christy changed into jeans and a sweatshirt, forced down another cup of coffee and looked out the kitchen window every third second.

Outwardly Taylor appeared unruffled, but Christy could tell from the pain that flashed in and out of her sister's face that the intensity of the contractions was increasing dramatically.

"I think it might be a good idea if you called the feed store. If Russ isn't there, then contact Cody."

"Great idea!" Christy leaped at the possibility of bringing someone else into the picture. The sooner the better. "Just a minute," she said. "Who's Cody?"

"Cody Franklin...he's the newly elected sheriff and a good friend. I don't know what his schedule is, so try the office first. If he's not there, his home number is written down in the front of the phone book."

Contacting anyone, including the National Guard, sounded like a stroke of brilliance to Christy. She found the impossibly thin phone book in the drawer. Good grief, she'd ordered from menus thicker than this.

While she was at it, Christy phoned the feed store. The lady who answered claimed Russ had left a half hour earlier, and she hadn't a clue where he'd gone next. Christy accepted this bit of information with a grain of salt. At the rate matters were developing, she was about to take an advanced course in childbirth.

Christy found the sheriff's home number right where Taylor claimed it would be. She punched out his number and waited impatiently for someone, anyone, to answer.

"Hello," a groggy voice answered on the fourth ring.

"Hi, oh, thank God you answered." Christy was so relieved, she wanted to weep. She sucked in one giant breath and rushed to explain. "You don't know me. I'm Christy Manning, Taylor Palmer's sister, and Russ left an hour ago and promised he'd be back before now and he isn't and Taylor's water broke and she's in labor. She keeps insisting she won't leave for the hospital until Russ comes home, but he isn't here, and frankly, I don't know that much about delivering babies."

A short silence followed. "Taylor's in labor?"

"That's what I just got done saying. The second and equally important factor is that Russ, the father of this about-to-be-born-baby, isn't here. He said he'd only be gone an hour, but he's late, and Taylor really should be leaving for the hospital."

"Where did he say he was going?"

"The feed store. But he left there thirty minutes ago and disappeared." That was a slight exaggeration, but the situation called for a minor stretching of the truth, although she realized she'd made it sound as if he'd been abducted by aliens.

"I'll find him and be there as soon as I can."

The relief that washed over Christy was like a cool evening rain after the hottest day of summer. Taylor needed her, and the last thing Christy wanted to do was reveal how frightened this situation was making her. She'd made this trip to help Taylor with the baby. As in diaper, hold, burp. *Not deliver.*

The next twenty minutes removed as many years from Christy's life span. She coaxed Taylor into the living room and had her lie down on the sofa. The ease with which Christy was able to do so spoke volumes about Taylor's condition. Although she struggled to disguise it, her dauntless older sister was frightened. The pains were far stronger than Taylor was willing to admit, and the fact that she labored to hide it from Christy truly concerned her.

A whole lifetime seemed to pass before Christy heard a car come barreling down the driveway. Taylor sighed visibly and relaxed against the wall of pillows Christy had placed behind her back. "That's Russ now."

Christy hurried toward the back door. She didn't recognize the car as Russ's, but that was the least of her worries. The four-wheel-drive Cherokee hadn't even come to a complete stop before her brother-in-law leaped out of the front seat.

He raced up the stairs, taking three at a time. "Where's Taylor?" he demanded.

Christy sagged with relief against the doorjamb and pointed toward the living room. She was about to follow her brother-in-law when a second man unfolded his long limbs and climbed out of the driver's seat.

For the life of her Christy couldn't pull her eyes away. It was all she could do not to throw her arms around him and thank him. "You must be Cody."

He touched the rim of his Stetson. "At your service. You must be Taylor's sister," he said, sauntering toward her.

"Christy Manning," she said authoritatively, as if she had the situation completely under control and frequently delivered babies while vacationing. With the precision a general would have admired, she stepped forward to offer the newly elected sheriff of Custer County her hand. In truth she was so grateful he'd found Russ that she was close to tears.

Not more than a few seconds later, Russ appeared, carrying Taylor. "You ready?" he demanded of his friend.

"Russ, put me down this instant," Taylor insisted. "I'm too heavy."

"We'll argue later, but at the moment you're about to give birth to my son," Russ reminded her, his face wreathed in a tight frown.

"Our baby could very well be a girl," Taylor contested. "You're still so pigheaded you refuse to—"

"I swear you're the only woman on God's green earth who would argue with me at a time like this."

"I'd think you'd be used to it by now," Taylor mumbled, and her voice faded as a fresh contraction overtook her. She closed her eyes, pressed her hands to her belly and breathed deeply.

Russ's distraught gaze connected with Christy's.

"I'll get her suitcase," Christy said as she rushed into the master bedroom. When she reappeared, Cody took the single bag from her hands and stuffed it inside the car. Taylor and Russ were situated in the back seat, and the passenger door was open and ready for Christy. Without another word, she climbed inside and snapped the seat belt into place.

The ride to the hospital took a full hour. Christy didn't need to look at the speedometer to know Cody was traveling well above the speed limit. If anything, she had to stop herself from pleading with him to go even faster.

Taylor did an admirable job of disguising the extent of her discomfort, but it was apparent to all that the sooner she was under medical supervision the better. Russ was wonderful, calm and collected.

The carburetor in Russ's truck had started acting up, and he'd pulled over to the side of the road to repair the problems. Cody had found him bent over the engine, trying to fix it so he could make it back to the ranch.

Christy held herself tense until they reached the outskirts of Miles City. Only then did she feel herself start to relax.

Within ten minutes of their arrival at the hospital, Taylor was in the labor room with Russ at her side. Cody and Christy were relegated to the waiting room, where they leafed through six-month-old issues of *Time* magazine.

Soon bored with those, Christy found her gaze wandering to Cody. Fine lines fanned out from the corners of his dark eyes, and sharply cut grooves bracketed his mouth. He was tanned, his skin weathered by the sun and wind. It was the type of rich bronze coloring that others strived to achieve under a sunlamp. His hair was thick and as dark as his eyes and cut military short. He wasn't handsome or stunning or anything else she could easily put a name to, but he was beyond a doubt the most uncompromisingly masculine man she'd ever seen. Immediately she experienced a faint stirring of guilt.

James. Dear, sweet James. Always so patient and understanding. She shouldn't even be looking at another man, not when she had James.

Cody glanced up from his magazine, and their eyes met. Christy did an admirable job of faking a smile. He returned the gesture and went back to reading. Christy made a pretense of doing the same thing. Despite her best efforts, she found her gaze wandering back to the sheriff. It was somewhat embarrassing to realize that it wasn't law and order that stuck in her mind when she looked at him. Cody Franklin was incredibly male. Incredibly incredible. Everything about him spoke of strength and determination: the way he walked, the square set of his jaw, even the way he sat with his ankle resting over his knee. Shaking herself as though from a deep sleep, she flipped through the pages of a two-year-old issue of *People*. Something was definitely wrong with her. No doubt it had to do with Taylor and the baby. Babies were said to stir up lots of feelings and buried emotions. The amazing part was that she should find this man so attractive.

Enough!

More determined than ever, Christy reached for another magazine and focused her attention away from the sheriff.

"I take it you just arrived in Cougar Point?" Cody surprised her by asking.

"Last night," Christy said, setting aside the dog-eared issue of *People*. "Actually, when I went to bed, it was early this morning. Russ left the house about the time I came down for coffee, and the next thing I knew, Taylor was telling me she was experiencing these 'funny' pains, only I wasn't laughing, and neither was she."

"How long after that did you phone me?"

"Too long," Christy said vehemently. "Taylor claimed the pains weren't anything to worry about. I knew at the time I should never have listened to her. Good grief, what does she know?"

Cody smiled, and her eyes were immediately drawn to the full sensual appeal of his mouth. Frustrated with herself, she quickly looked away.

"Don't be so hard on yourself. You handled the situation just the way you should have." His attention returned to the periodical. Christy reached for another herself, but when she glanced up, she found Cody studying her. "I don't mean to stare," he apologized, "but I can't get over how much you and Taylor resemble each other."

That was almost worthy of a laugh. She'd hardly been able to keep her eyes off Cody Franklin from the moment they arrived at the hospital, and he was apologizing for staring at her! As for the part about the two sisters looking alike, Christy took that as a supreme compliment. Taylor was stunning. In fact, Christy couldn't remember a time when her sister had been more exquisitely beautiful. Taylor was the beauty, not Christy. She didn't mean to sell herself short. She was reasonably attractive; comely was a word that drifted easily into her mind. Perhaps the only real difference was that Taylor had spunk. Her older sister had always displayed such tenacity, such mettle. When it came to dealing with their headstrong father, Taylor had more courage than a troop of Green Berets.

Anyone looking at the two sisters would know they were related; Christy was willing to grant the sheriff that much. Their deep blue eyes were a distinct family trait, shared by their three older brothers, as was the slightly turned-up-nose.

The two sisters styled their hair differently. Taylor chose to keep her thick chestnut hair long, whereas Christy preferred hers short, clipped above the ears in a breezy wash-and-wear style.

Christy was about to make some comment along the lines of what a peaceful community Cougar Point was when Russ appeared. His eyes were slightly dazed as he walked toward them. He paused and plowed his fingers through his hair with enough force to cause Christy to wince.

Cody and Christy stood as Russ approached.

"Taylor's ready to go into the delivery room."

"So soon?" Christy cried, her heart in her throat. "We just got here." She paused long enough to check her watch and swallow down a taste of panic over the might-have-beens. "We've only been here twenty minutes. How could she possibly be ready for the delivery room?"

"I don't know.... The nurse just told me the baby's about to be born."

"Of course. But it wasn't supposed to be this soon."

Russ wiped a hand down his face. "You're telling me? If Cody hadn't found me when he did..." He left the rest unsaid, but the implication was obvious.

Christy slumped back into the chair, her knees ready to buckle. From everything she'd read and heard, babies were supposed to take their sweet time, especially the first one. What about those twenty-hour labors her friends had described in minute detail? What about all the talk of first labors dragging on and on for days on end? Apparently Taylor hadn't been listening.

Russ returned to the double doors and paused, looking back into the waiting room. His Adam's apple worked up and down, and Christy realized if she'd been shaken by the news, it had affected Russ far more profoundly.

"Are you all right?" Cody asked.

"Of course," she lied. "I'm not the one who's having a baby minutes after I arrive at the hospital." A fact for which Christy was eternally grateful. She wasn't nearly as courageous as Taylor, either. In fact, when it came right down to it, she was simply a watered-down version of her older sister. All her life Christy had admired Taylor, wanting to be more like her. Instead, she was complacent and congenial, never causing her parents a moment's concern. Their father once claimed he owed every gray hair on his head to Taylor and every laugh line to Christy. His two daughters were the joy of his life.

"You look like you're about to faint," Cody said, watching her closely.

"Don't be ridiculous," she snapped, then instantly regretted her sharp tongue. She darted Cody an apologetic look.

"Come on," Cody suggested, "let's walk. It'll help pass the time."

"Pass what time?" she cried. "We haven't been here more than a few minutes, and already Taylor's being wheeled into the delivery room."

"Come on, you look like you need to get your blood circulating."

He was right, although Christy hated to admit it. Emotions were coming at her from every direction. Her first concern was for Taylor and the baby. The thought of this precious life, created in love, stirred awake a realm of deep feelings. Christy's stomach started churning, her palms sweated, and her heart did a jig of its own. She couldn't have uttered a word had her life depended on it.

They walked down the entire length of the wide hallway and stopped in front of the nursery. Christy paused to admire the single row of newborns swaddled in pink and blue blankets and unexpectedly found tears clouding in her eyes. Normally she wasn't sentimental or weepy. She didn't dare look over at Cody. He'd assume... She hadn't a clue what he'd assume, but it wouldn't be good.

"Christy?"

"The babies are really beautiful, aren't they?" she whispered, centering her gaze on the five newborns.

"Yes, they are," he answered softly. He stood behind her and pressed his hands on the curve of her shoulders. His touch was light, but it offered her a steadiness and comfort that had been sadly lacking all morning. He didn't say a word when she brushed the telltale moisture from her cheeks, and Christy was grateful.

She didn't know what had come over her in the past several hours. She turned to face Cody, placed her hands on his forearms and stared up at him, her eyes bright with unshed tears.

Nothing seemed real anymore. It was as if she were walking around in a dream. A living fantasy was beginning to unfold right before her. Perhaps she'd spent too many hours on the road. Obviously she had. Otherwise she wouldn't be looking into the darkest pair of brown eyes she'd ever seen and thinking the things she was thinking.

Cody was staring at her with the same wonder and surprise that had gripped her. It seemed as if he was about to say something important when the doors at the other end of the hall opened and Russ, wearing a green surgical gown and pants, stepped out. A large smile dominated his face. Seeing him, both Christy and Cody rushed forward.

"It's a boy," Russ announced, his eyes shimmering with tears. He let out a wild shout of joy, gripped a shocked Christy around the waist and boisterously whirled her around.

"Congratulations," Cody said, stepping forward. The two men exchanged hearty handshakes, then hugged, slapping each other hard across the back.

Russ didn't speak for several moments and seemed to be composing himself. "He weighed in at eight pounds, three ounces, and he's the ugliest little critter you've ever seen. Taylor kept saying how beautiful he is, and all I could see was this furious pink face bawling as loud as anything I've ever heard. His legs were pumping the air like an oil rig. That boy is madder than a wet wasp."

Christy felt tears crowd her eyes as she pressed her fingertips to her lips. "How's Taylor?"

"She's fine...more than fine. Heaven almighty, that woman's incredible. I don't know what I ever did that was good enough to deserve her, but I intend to thank God every day of my life." He ran the back of his hand under his nose and started walking backward. "I've got to get back. They're taking Eric into the nursery now, and the delivery room nurse said I could go back there and watch him being washed and dressed. If I have anything to say about it, I'll do the washing and dressing myself."

"You're naming him Eric?" Christy asked as she moved one step forward.

Russ nodded. "Eric Russell, after your father and me. Taylor insists."

"That sounds like a perfectly wonderful name to me," Christy whispered, surprised at the way the emotion clogged her throat. Her father would be so proud, the buttons would pop right off his shirt.

"If you two walk over to the nursery, you might be able to see him, too," Russ added excitedly. "Taylor will be out of the delivery room anytime now. I know she'll want to talk to you both, so stick around for a little bit, okay?''

Christy and Cody had already started in that direction when Russ stopped them. "Hey, one last thing. Taylor and I talked it over, and we want the two of you to be Eric's godparents."

Christy exchanged a meaningful glance with Cody before they simultaneously nodded.

"We'd be honored," Cody answered for them.

"Truly honored," Christy repeated, her throat tightening all the more.

Russ disappeared, and in her excitement Christy whirled around to face Cody, only she didn't realize he was quite so close. She flattened her hands against his chest as she smiled up at him, her joy overflowing now that her nephew had been born.

Cody looked down on her and returned the smile. He was so close, so warm. She could see every line, every pore of his skin, every individual hair of his eyelashes. His dark eyes were alive with emotion.

Slowly, moving as if he were hypnotized, Cody slipped his arms around her waist and raised her from the ground. Her hands clutched his shirt collar as his eyes delved into hers.

"I believe congratulations are in order, don't you?"

"Yes," she said, hugging him close, afraid he meant to kiss her, equally fearing he wouldn't.

How would she ever explain kissing another man to James? How would she ever be able to rationalize allowing Cody to hold her like this when she'd promised to spend her life loving someone else?

Chapter Two

"Oh, Taylor, he's so beautiful," Christy said through the emotion-filled lump blocking her throat. "Russ held him for me to see and..." She paused, unable to continue. The minute she'd seen Eric, her heart had swollen with such a profound sense of love that it had been impossible to hold back the tears.

"You're crying," Taylor accused softly.

Christy nodded and smeared the moisture across the arch of her cheeks. She reached for her sister, and the two hugged spontaneously. This incredible wealth of emotion took Christy by storm, bombarding her with a host of sensations from all sides.

"I love you, Taylor. I really do. And I love Eric, too. He's beautiful, perfect. I feel so happy." She straightened and gave a breathy laugh. "I want to throw open the windows and tell the word my sister just gave birth to a beautiful baby boy."

"Did you get a chance to talk to Mom and Dad?"

Christy nodded. The moment her mother heard the news she'd started weeping for joy and her father had taken the phone. His own voice hadn't sounded all that steady, either. Russ had done most of the talking. When it was her turn, Christy was convinced she'd jabbered on like a magpie, but she couldn't seem to stop herself.

Following the conversation, Russ and Cody had gone out to the hospital gift shop to buy a box of cigars. Christy had been left to spend these few moments alone with her sister.

"I'm sorry I frightened you so badly," Taylor said apologetically, "but I didn't want to leave for the hospital without Russ."

"I understood. Don't worry." On the contrary, Christy had been nearly frantic, but it didn't matter now that everything had turned out so well.

Her sister sighed softly. "I'm glad you were able to meet Cody."

At the mention of the other man's name, Christy abruptly looked away, feeling uneasy. She hadn't had the chance to tell Taylor and Russ about her engagement to James Wilkens. Unfortunately the diamond ring James had given her was still at the jeweler's being sized. If she had been wearing the ring, it would have been a natural lead-in to her announcement. She'd meant to surprise her sister and brother-in-law with the big news the moment she'd arrived, but it had been so late and everyone was exhausted. Then, before Christy knew it, it was morning and Taylor had gone into labor.

Now the timing was all wrong. Tomorrow, she promised herself, she'd tell Taylor when everything was a little less hectic. Even as she formed the thought, Christy hesitated, not fully understanding why.

Her head spun to the wild beating of her heart and her thoughts skidded to a blunt halt. Who did she think she was fooling?

She did know why.

Cody Franklin had hugged her when Russ had come to tell them about Eric. Even now, an hour later, the way she'd felt in his arms still caused her pulse to accelerate. He'd pulled her close, and the feeling of being held by this man was completely and utterly natural, as instinctive as breathing or sleeping. It was as if they'd known each other all their lives. As if their relationship was one of long standing.

Without his uttering a word, Christy knew he'd experienced the same lavish range of sensations. For the longest moment they'd stared blatantly at each other, neither speaking. If Russ hadn't been there, Christy couldn't help wondering what would have happened. What they would have said to each other. If anything.

But Russ had been there, and after an awkward moment, Cody had released her. He'd dropped his arms with a reluctance that sent blood pounding through her veins until she grew dizzy simply remembering.

James was her fiancé! Even now she had to struggle to bring the attorney to mind. Her parents had been thrilled with the news of their engagement, but then Christy had known they would be. Her father had told her often enough James would make her an excellent husband. They'd been dating off and on for nearly two years, almost from the first week Christy had been hired as a paralegal at James's law firm. Their relationship, however, hadn't turned serious until three months ago. Until then, their dates had been casual get-togethers with mutual friends. Then they'd started working together on an important case. It had been a real coup for James to be assigned to defend Mr. Mulligan against the Internal Revenue Service, and if everything went well, it could mean a partnership for him.

"Christy?"

She returned her attention to her sister. "Sorry. Were you saying something?"

"I was just mentioning how pleased I was that you met Cody."

"He...seems very nice," Christy answered, and almost sighed with relief when the nurse walked into the room, distracting her sister's attention from the subject of the sheriff. The woman brought in a huge bouquet of red roses in a tall crystal vase.

"Oh, my," Taylor breathed, reaching for the card. She tore open the small envelope and read the message. Immediate tears filled her eyes as she held the card to her breast. "They're from Russ."

"How sweet."

Taylor smiled softly as a faraway look came into her eyes. Christy speculated her sister was remembering the first time she'd met Russ and all that had transpired since. Russ may not have been the man her family would have chosen for Taylor to marry, but one fact had been clear from the instant they flew to Seattle to attend their parents' anniversary party. Russ Palmer loved Taylor. Beyond question. Beyond doubt. Whatever reservations Christy and her brothers held regarding the rancher and this marriage had been quickly dissolved.

Footsteps from behind Christy told her Russ and Cody had returned.

"Russ . . ." Taylor held out her arms to her husband.
"The roses are so beautiful. Thank you."

Christy's brother-in-law walked across the room, and
his eyes drifted closed as he took his wife into his arms.
He whispered something in her ear, and Taylor smiled
softly and nodded. The scene was an intimate one, and
Christy felt like an intruder. She backed away, avoiding looking at Cody until it was impossible not to.

"Hello, again," he greeted, and his voice was low and
rumbling. His smile contained a warmth and depth that
multiplied a hundredfold all the sensations she'd experienced earlier, the very feelings she was trying to put
out of her mind. Once again Christy was struck by the
possessiveness she experienced looking at him, studying him. For the past hour she'd been trying to put a
name to why she should feel anything toward him.
Nothing had come to her. No understanding. No in-
sights. Nothing.

They were little more than strangers, and yet she felt
as comfortable with him as if she'd known him all her
life. At the same time, he rattled her composure unlike
anyone she'd ever met. It seemed absurdly ironic to be
so flustered by a man and at the same time feel so shel-
tered.

Cody glanced toward Russ and Christy. "Would you
like to go down to the nursery and view our godson?"

She nodded, gladly accepting an excuse to leave Taylor and Russ alone.

Together they walked down the familiar corridor until they stood in front of the large nursery window. But
it wasn't the newborns that captured their attention.
They'd make a comment about one baby or the other,
but it was each other that interested them most. After a

while they gave up the pretense of looking at the newborns and simply stared at one another.

"Russ phoned the ranch and is having a couple of his hands drive a car over for him," Cody said after a while. "The way he talked, he's planning to spend the day with Taylor."

Once more Christy nodded. It seemed all she was capable of doing. Being this close to Cody was akin to being trapped in a magnetic force field. It didn't matter how much she resisted, he drew her attention to him and held it, sapping whatever strength she possessed.

With a determined effort, she diverted her attention to Eric. The infant was sleeping comfortably, swaddled in a pale blue receiving blanket. A long-sleeved T-shirt covered his tiny arms and fists. He was so small, so incredibly precious.

Cody's gaze followed hers, and when he spoke, his voice was filled with astonishment. "He's really something, isn't he?"

"Yes." Her voice came out sounding like a lacy whisper. "And to think we could have ended up delivering him."

"We?" Cody joked. "In all my years of law enforcement I've been spared that. Thank God."

Standing behind her, Cody's large hands cupped her shoulders naturally, as if he'd been holding and touching her for a lifetime. It felt right and good to have this man so close. A small shudder skimmed down her spine at the innocent contact, and briefly she shut her eyes.

Cody must have felt something, because he turned her around to face him, his own eyes narrowing slightly. "You're trembling."

She couldn't deny it. This man she barely knew confused her, bewildered her. The worst part of all this suspended emotion was that she couldn't understand the reason why. She'd met and dated any number of attractive, compelling men before. Yet none of them had ever overwhelmed her the way Cody did.

"Are you cold?"

"No," she answered quickly, flustered by his questions.

"What's wrong?"

How could she possibly explain something to him she couldn't fully understand herself. "Nothing."

His eyes found hers, and she could have sworn they went several shades darker. "Does this happen often?"

"No," she denied vehemently. "Does it to you?" Christy swallowed, astonished she'd had the courage to ask him such a personal question.

"No," he answered after a moment. "Never."

Abruptly she pulled her gaze away, baffled all the more by his openness. His honesty. It was exactly what she'd longed to hear. And what she'd feared.

"I . . . I need to get back to the ranch," she said, seeking an excuse to do something, anything to end this heightened awareness between them. "Taylor asked me to make some phone calls for her."

Cody lowered his gaze from her eyes to her lips. His look, unhurried and sensual, was as intimate as a kiss. Christy's stomach became a churning mass of doubts mingled with an abundance of misgivings. She'd like to blame this feeling on the chaotic events of the day.

Slowly, almost unaware of what she was doing, Christy raised her eyes to meet Cody's. He didn't look too comfortable. If anything, he seemed as perplexed and hesitant as she.

"I need to get back myself," he murmured.

Not until that moment did Christy realize the only way she had of returning to Cougar Point was with Cody. A sinking feeling assailed her. There was no way for her to avoid an hour or more with him in the intimate confines of his Cherokee.

Cody Franklin had no idea what was happening between him and his best friend's sister-in-law. To be honest, he hadn't paid Christy Manning much attention until they were sitting in the hospital waiting room. She'd been terribly agitated, flipping through one magazine, and then without pause, reaching for another. Cody sincerely doubted she'd read a single word.

Then Russ had appeared and announced Taylor was ready for the delivery room, and Cody had watched as Christy quickly started to unravel.

He'd suggested they take a short walk in an effort to help her relax. She'd seemed fragile and anxious. He didn't know how much comfort he would be to her, since he was a stranger, but the least he could do was try. He'd had enough experience from his years as a lawman to suggest some physical activity to help take her mind off her sister.

It was when they'd stopped to look at the babies in the nursery that Cody had experienced the faint stirring of something more. Faint stirring, hell, it was like a fist to his gut!

From that moment on something had started to awaken deep within him. He experienced a lost sensation, as if he were charting unknown land, and each turn led him farther away from all that was familiar. He was at a loss for words, feeling as tongue-tied as a callow youth. It had been in his mind to involve her in conversation, occupy her with inane questions about

Seattle and her job, whatever he could to keep her from thinking about Taylor. Only he hadn't made a single query.

Every time Cody started to speak, he found himself lost in her eyes. He'd never seen a woman with eyes this color of china blue. They reminded him of the coldest days of winter, when everything around him eagerly anticipated the promise of spring. When she smiled, those same blue eyes brightened even more, and it was like watching sunshine slice through the rain.

She'd look at him, and Cody swore he could see all the way to her soul. She was guileless and genuine and so incredibly lovely, it was all he could do to keep from staring at her, a fact he'd already apologized for once that day.

Twice he'd placed his hands on her shoulders. It wasn't his habit to comfort women, and he was at a loss to understand his own actions even now. The first time he'd held her, she'd obviously been shaken by Russ's news about Taylor, and he'd reached out in an effort to steady her.

The moment his hands had closed over her shoulders, his heart had started beating like a runaway train. The last time anything like that had happened he'd been thirteen and had kissed a girl for the first time. As a youth he'd felt like pitching a baseball into outer space, running like the wind and shouting at the top of his lungs.

Twenty years had passed, and the impact had been nearly as strong. Sweet heaven, what was happening to him? Every minute with her he learned something more about himself, and every emotion he discovered only served to bewilder him more.

"I'm sorry if it's an inconvenience for you to take me to the ranch," Christy said, sliding into the front seat of his four-wheel drive.

"It isn't any problem." The only difficulty it created was one of his own making. He was caught in some mysterious caldron of yearning. Perhaps, in some strange way, all this had to do with Russ and Taylor. He couldn't help envying the happiness his friends had found. Taylor was the best thing that had ever happened to Russ Palmer. Now Russ was a father.

Cody paused, half expecting to feel a twinge of jealousy or resentment. When he'd first been introduced to Taylor, he'd wanted to date her himself, but she'd already met Russ and it was clear she was falling in love with the rancher. Cody had stood on the sidelines and watched their romance unfold, amused at the way they'd both fought it so hard.

No, jealousy hadn't promoted these feelings; he was convinced of that. The only emotion he experienced for his friends following the birth of their son was a pure sense of shared happiness.

The drive, which had seemed like four hundred miles earlier in the day with Taylor and Russ in the back seat, took no time whatsoever on the return. Christy said little, but neither seemed uneasy with the silence. Occasionally Cody would look over to her, and their gazes would meld. Each time it happened, something magical, something magnetic would pass involuntarily between them. After a while it became a challenge to discover what it was that fascinated him so much about Taylor's sister, and he found his gaze repeatedly drawn as he attempted to analyze the situation.

She was a pretty thing, but no prettier than any number of women he'd dated. Not as beautiful as

Becca. He paused, surprised that he didn't immediately experience a prickle of pain as he thought of the other woman. It had been three years now since Becca had turned his life upside down. He tried not to think of her at all, to push her to the farthest reaches of his mind as though he'd never known her, never loved her. For the most part he succeeded . . . for the most part.

"Would you like to stop off and get something to eat?" Cody found himself asking as they neared Cougar Point. He wasn't so hungry as he was reluctant to leave her.

By all rights Cody should have been exhausted. He'd had only a couple of hours of sleep in the past forty-eight. Instead he felt alive, reborn, and he had yet to understand the implications of that.

All he knew was that he'd met a woman, a warm, caring, generous woman, and he felt like he was sixteen years old all over again.

"I'm starved," Christy returned enthusiastically. "I was so concerned about Taylor this morning that I forgot to eat breakfast."

"I haven't had anything, either."

"I got you out of bed when I phoned, didn't I?"

Cody nodded. Hell, he'd give his right hand to have her sweet voice wake him every morning. "I worked the graveyard shift last night."

"You must be exhausted."

On the contrary, Cody had never felt more vital. "Not at all," he said, mustering a small smile to reassure her. "There are a couple of decent restaurants in town, but if you're interested in breakfast, the best place to eat is the bowling alley."

"Great."

Cody had expected her to laugh or to question his choice. She was, after all, a city girl, and he sincerely doubted that anyone in Seattle had ever taken her out to eat at a bowling alley. But she accepted his choice enthusiastically.

Since it was midafternoon by this time, the parking lot was nearly deserted. Christy didn't wait for him to come around and open the door for her, a fact that didn't surprise him. Taylor hadn't waited for him to open her door the one time he'd taken her out, either.

Cody chose a booth toward the back of the restaurant and slid into the red upholstered seat. Christy sat across from him and reached for the menu, which was tucked between the sugar bowl and the salt and pepper shakers.

"Howdy, Cody," Mary Andrews said as she stepped to the table, carrying two water glasses. She glanced curiously at Christy.

"This is Taylor's sister, Christy Manning."

"I don't suppose Taylor had her baby, did she?"

Christy's eyes softened as she nodded. "This morning. Eric Russell Palmer weighed in at eight pounds, three ounces."

Mary grinned from ear to ear. "That's great. You don't mind if I let folks know, do you?"

Christy shook her head. "Please do."

Still grinning, Mary pulled a small green pad from her apron pocket. "What can I get for you two?"

"I'll have the breakfast special," Christy said, closing her menu.

"So will I," Cody said, tucking his own back into place.

Mary wrote down their order, then walked back to the kitchen.

For a long time Cody said nothing. Partly because he didn't know what to say and partly because he didn't feel the need to fill the void with small talk. He was comfortable with Christy. He hadn't felt that way with any woman, ever. He looked over at her and wondered if she was experiencing this same sense of serenity, and instinctively knew she was. "What are you thinking?" he asked.

She smiled, and her expression warmed even more with the action. "If we're Eric's godparents, does that mean the two of us are related?"

A grin lit his face. "I suppose it does. I'm just not sure how."

"Me, neither."

One thing he did know: the idea of being linked to Christy pleased him immeasurably. "Tell me about yourself." He wanted to know everything there was about her from the time she was in preschool to the present.

"I'm the youngest of five."

"Spoiled?"

"Terribly."

He deliberately drew his gaze away from her mouth, which had fascinated him for several minutes. Beyond question, he knew he was going to kiss her. He didn't know when. Soon, if possible. Nor did he know where. Only that the need to taste her was quickly becoming an obsession.

"What about you?" Christy asked, pulling a napkin from the holder and spreading it across her lap, taking time to smooth it out. She seemed to be avoiding eye contact with him. That didn't surprise Cody. He'd been blatantly staring at her every chance he got. Her mouth enthralled him as nothing ever had. Soft. Pink. Moist. Just right for kissing. Just right for tasting.

"What about you?" she repeated, and the question seemed to echo loudly in the thick silence.

"I was born in Miles City," he said, focusing instead on the tabletop, confident he was embarrassing her. "In the same hospital as Eric, as a matter of fact."

"Was your father a rancher?"

"No. He was a lawman, just as his father was before him. The Franklins have a long tradition of upholding law and order in Custer County."

"Did you always want to work for the Sheriff's Department?"

"Always. For as long as I can remember I dreamed of wearing a badge."

"How proud they must be of you," she said in a way that caused his heart to quicken. What she was said was true. But his father and grandfather would never know he'd been elected sheriff; his two younger sisters were the only members of his family left.

Cody didn't want to talk about himself, not when there was so much to learn about her. "What did you want to be when you were a kid?"

"Not a paralegal," she said, then looked away, as if the words had slipped out before she could check what she'd said. "I didn't even know what one was until high school. Sad to say, my dreams were far more traditional. I wanted to be a mommy."

"And now?"

"And now," she repeated in a whisper, frowning.

She was saved from having to answer him by Mary, who delivered two oblong platters to their table. Each was heaped high with steaming hash browns, scrambled eggs, sausage and toast.

Their conversation ceased as they both reached for their forks. Neither spoke for several moments.

"I don't think I realized how hungry I was," Christy admitted, reaching for the small container of jelly. She peeled back the cover and scooped out the preserves with her knife.

"Where's Mandy?" Cody asked, remembering Russ's teenage sister, who lived with Russ and Taylor, for the first time that day.

"She's with a friend. Russ phoned from the hospital and let her know about Eric first thing. She seemed to be filled with questions and was sorry she missed all the excitement."

Cody pushed his empty plate aside. Mary stopped off at the table to refill their coffee mugs and take away Cody's plate.

"You might as well take mine, too," Christy said, leaning back in the booth. She placed her hands over her flat stomach and sighed. "I can't believe I ate all that."

"Can I get you anything more?" Mary asked.

"Nothing, thanks," Cody answered for them.

Mary set the bill on the table, grinned and walked away.

They left the restaurant a few minutes later. Cody opened the door for Christy, insisting on the small courtesy because he enjoyed doing something, however small, for her.

She seemed preoccupied and anxious on the ride out to the Lazy P. He started to ask her what time she'd arrived the night before, but even before he'd finished the question, he knew she wasn't listening.

"I'm sorry. Did you say something?" she asked, glancing at him.

"It wasn't important." He pulled off the main road and headed down the long, dusty driveway. This time of year the road was filled with ruts deep enough to send them both bouncing around the interior of his Cherokee if he wasn't careful to watch where he was driving. In several spots he slowed down to a snail's pace. Then he was forced to ask himself if he was concerned about his car or the fact the sooner he arrived at the ranch, the sooner he'd have to leave Christy.

Once he reached the ranch yard, he turned off the engine and climbed out of the cab. Christy had opened the car door, offering him just the excuse he needed to touch her. His hands located her slim waist as he lifted her down.

She hadn't been expecting his help and, caught off guard, she fell forward. She made a small sound as her hands made contact with his chest.

Neither moved. Cody couldn't believe how incredibly good it felt to have her in his arms again.

"I'm sorry," she said quickly, sounding winded.

"I'm not." Cody never had been one to beat around the bush, as the saying went. "Not in the least sorry," he reiterated.

Her hands were flattened against his chest, and he wondered if she could feel how hard his heart was beating, wondered if she had half an inkling of what he was feeling.

"Thanks for breakfast and the ride home," she murmured, but made no effort to move away from him.

Heat radiated from where her hands were touching him, warming him in ways he couldn't understand, but didn't question. She bunched her fingers as if to pull away, but if that was her intention, she didn't follow through.

Cody raised his hand to the side of her neck. His fingers stroked the kitten-soft skin there, and he watched, fascinated as she slowly closed her eyes.

Once more his gaze sought her mouth. Her lush, vulnerable mouth. Never had it looked more inviting than it did at that moment.

It seemed only natural to kiss her. Hell, he'd been thinking about doing exactly that for hours, but now that the opportunity presented itself, he hesitated. It was as if an inborn defense mechanism flashed a warning through his system. Kiss Christy Manning and you'll never be the same again, it seemed to be saying.

But the words of caution were all for naught. Cody couldn't have stopped himself to save his own life. Whatever came after, whatever fate life held for him, whatever the cost, he was going to kiss this woman.

Unhurriedly, deliberately, he pressed his lips over hers. She murmured something, and Cody felt the movement against his mouth, but it mattered little. If she were protesting, or if she were endorsing the kiss, he would never know.

Her lips were everything Cody dreamed they would be. Warm. Moist. Devastating. With a soft whimper she responded immediately, flowering open to him unselfishly in a way that made him want to protect her all his life. It was if he'd never kissed a woman before this moment. Never held one in his arms, or experienced anything this extraordinary.

Her arms made their way around his neck as she leaned into him. Her softness melded into his hardness. She was remarkably soft. As soft as a whisper. As soft as a feather bed.

White-hot sensation seemed to explode inside him. Cody kissed her again and again, his hands in her hair, cupping the back of her head. He kissed her until his breathing became labored and hard. Until he heard her moan, and then realized it was his own sigh of longing that echoed in his ears. Still he didn't release her. Still he held her against him, never wanting to let her go.

Only when Christy stiffened did Cody slacken his hold. Slowly he opened his eyes to discover her looking up at him, her beautiful eyes bright with tears. He frowned until he understood. Then, in a heartbeat, he knew. The kissing had affected her as profoundly as it had him.

"I know what you're thinking," he whispered, tucking his finger under her chin, dropping his mouth to hers, unable to resist her.

"You don't," she denied. "You couldn't possibly know."

"But I do," he countered. "You're thinking this is the craziest thing that's ever happened to you. I know because that's exactly what I'm thinking. We barely know each other, and yet I feel as if I've known you all my life."

Her eyes widened briefly as if his words had accurately hit their mark.

"We don't know each other," she confirmed. "All this is because of Taylor and Russ. Their happiness, their joy and excitement must be rubbing off on us. Don't you see how foolish this is?"

"No." He didn't mean to be blunt or obtuse. He was nearly thirty-five years old and long past the age of game playing. Christy was several years younger, but she knew. The same way he did. She may choose to deny it, but he wouldn't.

"Are you saying you didn't want me to kiss you?" he asked, trusting her to be honest, because he didn't believe she could be anything else.

It took her several moments to answer him, and when she did her voice was uneven and raspy. "That's the problem.... I've never wanted anything more."

Chapter Three

Christy woke early the next morning after a restless night's sleep. She'd tossed and turned so rambunctiously that the sheets had been pulled loose from the bottom of the bed and the bedspread had slipped all the way onto the floor. Staring up at the ceiling, Christy slowly expelled her breath while mulling over the events of the day before.

So much had happened.

Taylor's son had been born, and Christy had been introduced to the newly elected sheriff of Custer County.

However, Christy had more than *met* Cody Franklin. He'd taken her to breakfast late in the afternoon, and when he dropped her off at the ranch, he'd kissed her—and she'd let him. More than *let* him; she'd encouraged him. What she'd told him had been true. She'd never wanted anyone's kiss more.

Admitting as much certainly wasn't one of her more intelligent moves, but then it hadn't been her mind doing the talking. It had been her heart.

Once again she tried to focus her thoughts on James. He'd been so sweet the evening he'd given her the engagement ring. They'd gone out to eat, sitting at the dinner table with candlelight flickering and soft music playing in the background. Christy noticed that he'd barely touched his dinner. He seemed nervous, agitated, then he'd started talking nonstop. Normally James was a quiet man. It took a great deal to ruffle him. He'd been rambling for fifteen minutes or so, and Christy hadn't a clue where the discussion had been leading. She told him as much. Then James had gotten terribly flustered, and it was so unlike him.

Before Christy completely understood what was happening, James pulled a ring box from the inside of his suit pocket. He'd been so endearing, so wonderfully sweet as he held out the diamond, letting the ring speak for him.

By then Christy had become so flustered herself that all she could do was stare at the lovely solitary diamond glittering up at her. James had withdrawn it from its velvet bed, and without a word she'd lifted her hand and given it to him.

The entire transaction hadn't taken more than a couple of seconds. She'd promised to become his wife, promised to pledge her life to him without there ever being a word about love spoken between them. James cared for her, Christy felt assured of it. He wouldn't have given her the ring if he didn't. By the same token, she loved him. Otherwise she wouldn't have accepted his proposal.

Afterward, James had been ecstatic as he'd hugged and kissed her. The ring was too large and had nearly slipped off her finger as she'd shown it to her parents that same night. Both Eric and Elizabeth Manning had been thrilled with the news of Christy's engagement to the up-and-coming attorney.

It hadn't been until two days later, just before she left to drive to Montana, that the first of the doubts had come. She loved James, she reminded herself, repeating it again and again on the long drive across three states.

James was a quiet man, a good man. He'd been a friend long before they'd become romantically involved, and from everything she'd read, friends made the very best husbands.

Perhaps the most convincing argument for this marriage was how comfortable Christy felt with him. Her parents thought the world of James. They seemed more excited than she was about the prospect of him joining the family. Her father talked of little else, reminding Christy that she was his sunshine, Daddy's darling girl. He promised her the wedding of the year.

But if she'd been experiencing a few niggling doubts before she left Seattle, they'd multiplied a hundredfold since she'd arrived in Montana and met Cody Franklin.

Cody.

His name went through her mind with the speed of a laser beam. For more reasons than she dared explore, she struggled to push every thought of the sheriff from her mind.

With a determination born of pride and a sense of fairness and truth that had been ingrained in her from birth, Christy tossed aside the sheet, climbed out of bed and dressed, determined to tell Russ, tell someone, anyone, about her engagement.

Russ, however, had already left the house. A note addressed to her was propped against the sugar bowl in the middle of the kitchen table. Taylor's husband briefly explained he would be with his men that morning, and she shouldn't look for him before noon. He also wrote that he wouldn't be able to visit Taylor and the baby until that evening. He signed off, then added that Christy should make herself at home.

Defeat settled over Christy like a thick mist, dampening her determination and her spirits. She couldn't keep quiet about herself and James much longer and still hold her head high.

It took only an hour for her to straighten up the house. She cooked herself something to eat, then realized she wasn't hungry. Russ, on the other hand, looked as if he'd fixed himself a breakfast large enough to feed five men. He'd made a minimal effort to clean the kitchen, but it was apparent he'd been in a rush.

With time on her hands, Christy wandered outside, wanting to investigate what she could of the ranch grounds. Since Russ was visiting Taylor that evening, she decided to drive to the hospital that afternoon.

A couple of hands paused and stared at her when she appeared.

"Good morning," Christy greeted cheerfully.

"Howdy." The lanky cowboy straightened and touched the rim of his hat, sauntering toward her. A fistful of cigars with pale blue bands was sticking out of his shirt pocket, evidence of Russ's eagerness to spread the news of his son's birth.

"You must be part of Mrs. Palmer's family."

"Christy Manning," she said, holding out her hand. "I'm Taylor's sister."

The middle-aged man took pains to remove his thick leather glove and clasped her soft palm in his callused one. "I'm pleased to make your acquaintance. Russ is out this morning, but I suspect he'll be back soon. Most folks call me Billy Joe."

"I'm pleased to meet you, Billy Joe," Christy said, looking toward the barn. Several horses stuck their sleek heads out of the upper part of the stall doors, glancing at her with open curiosity.

"If you'll excuse me," Billy Joe said, backing away from her. A chestnut gelding was saddled and prancing about, anxious to be on his way.

"Of course. I'm sorry. I didn't mean to hold you up."

"No problem." The ranch hand mounted the gelding in a single smooth motion. Christy couldn't help but admire the gracefulness of his movements. Pulling back on the stirrups, Billy Joe nodded toward her once more, then galloped out of the yard.

Left to her own devices, Christy wandered toward the barn, pausing in front of the first stall. The name Shadow was burned into a wood plaque above the door.

"Howdy, Shadow," Christy said, sticking the tips of her fingers into the tiny pockets near the waistband of her jeans. "You look like a friendly horse." Friendly enough, at any rate, for her to venture petting his long nose. She'd stroked it a couple of times while the gelding took pride in revealing his teeth and nickered his approval.

Seeing a large barrel of grain toward the middle of the barn, Christy stepped over to it, intending to reach for a handful of oats. She didn't know much about horses, but figured a handful of oats was sure to win approval.

"I thought I might find you in here," a deep male voice said from the front of the barn.

Christy's heart shot to her throat. Cody. She turned and found him silhouetted against the morning sunlight. Tall, lean and dark. He wore jeans and a western shirt with a string tie and was so strikingly handsome that for a moment all she could do was stare.

"Hello," she said, returning to her task, her hands trembling. It wasn't fair that he should have this effect on her. But then she was learning that little in life was fair.

Her fist loaded with grain, she walked back to Shadow's stall, hoping her steps didn't reveal her reluctance or her regret.

"Be sure to feed that to him with your palm flat, otherwise he might inadvertently bite you," Cody warned, moving toward her.

Christy was grateful for the advice and did as he suggested. Shadow ate the oats in quick order, and when he'd finished, Christy wiped her hand clean on her jean-clad thigh. Her heart was hammering so hard and fast, she was certain Cody could hear it.

"Did you sleep well?"

"No," she answered honestly. Her back was to him, but that was little help. She felt warm and dizzy just knowing he was there.

"I couldn't, either." His voice was soft and raspy. Sensual. "I only had a couple of hours of sleep the night before. By all that's right, I should have fallen asleep the minute my head touched the pillow. But I didn't. I couldn't."

Christy found a strange comfort in knowing his rest had been as unsettled as her own. "I...tossed and turned most of the night, then finally drifted off toward morning.''

"Me, too."

He'd left her the night before, and as she'd stood just inside the house and watched him drive away, a restless, brooding feeling had come over her. It hadn't dissipated until the moment he'd stepped into the barn. Cody spoke, and instantly the emptiness had started to leave her, as if everything had been set back into order once more.

Only it wasn't right. Everything was wrong, very wrong.

"We need to talk."

"Yes," she whispered. He was here, and it was as if her anxious vigil was over. She'd meant to tell Russ about James, knowing her brother-in-law would be sure to mention the fact to Cody. But this was better, much better. She could tell Cody herself. Explain before either of them was hurt. Before matters went too far.

Honesty was the best policy. She'd grown up believing it. Practicing it.

Christy was searching for just the right words, irritated with herself for not having thought this out more carefully beforehand. There should be an easy way to say it. The truth shouldn't be this difficult.

Then Cody stepped behind her, so close she could feel the heat radiating from his body. His hands settled over her shoulders, his touch feathery, and warm and reassuring. Slowly he turned her around so she faced him.

Their eyes locked, and Christy's throat went tight. His were beautiful, as dark and rich as Louisiana coffee. They were the eyes of a man who'd only recently learned to dream. Wistful eyes. Pensive eyes.

"Every time I'd try to sleep, all I could think about was you." He said it as if he was admitting to a misdeed, as if he'd struggled long and hard against allowing her to dominate his thoughts.

"It was the same with me." She shouldn't have told him that. Shouldn't admit his effect on her in one breath and then tell him about James in the other. "I—"

"I couldn't stop thinking about how good you felt in my arms. Too damn good."

She knew exactly what he was saying because she'd experienced the same thing herself. He felt good to her, too, the kind of good that made everything feel right, even when it was wrong. The kind of good that never diminished, never ceased.

"You felt it, too, didn't you?" He seemed to need confirmation from her.

She gave it reluctantly, breathlessly, lowering her eyes. "Yes."

They lapsed into silence then, as though neither of them knew what more to say. There didn't seem to be a need for words. Christy knew what Cody was thinking and feeling as clearly as if he'd spoken.

I need to kiss you again and discover if last night was real. He asked her with his eyes.

No, her heart cried. She couldn't allow it, couldn't deal with it. If Cody kissed her again, she'd be forced to confront issues she dared not face. Cody Franklin was a stranger. James was her fiancé. Her friend.

I've frightened you.

No, came the cry from the farthest corner of her heart. *Yes,* she countered almost immediately. Cody stirred emotions she didn't know she was capable of feeling. Emotions she'd never experienced with any man. Each time they were together, she became aware of him with ever-increasing intensity. This shouldn't be happening to her. Not now. Not ever. She was engaged to another man.

Frowning, almost as if he were unsure of himself, Cody took one step toward her. Christy's heart surged.

Don't, please, don't, she pleaded silently. *I can't refuse you. I can't refuse myself.*

But Cody had apparently given up listening to the cries of her heart. When she dared to look at him, she found him both watchful and silent.

Before another moment could pass, he reached for her, and whatever resistance she'd been able to muster burst like a mature dandelion in the wind. His mouth found hers, smooth and firm against her softness. She moaned in protest, but her small cry soon became a sigh of welcome, of need, of pleasure.

A tenderness blossomed within her, the sensations so exquisite they shocked her even more than they had a day earlier. It shouldn't be this good, this wonderful, she told herself over and over, wanting to weep with frustration. Yet it was better than anything she'd ever experienced.

Cody continued to worship her with his mouth, sliding his moist lips over hers in a wide, circular pattern, creating a delicate friction that left Christy clinging to him.

"I can't believe this," Cody murmured, and her mind echoed his words. She was struggling with reality, and felt both lost and weak.

Cody angled his head and dropped a succession of kisses down her neck and along the underside of her jaw until she moaned. He responded with a small, throaty sound of his own and quickly joined their mouths again, kissing hers lightly, softly, until her lips parted, welcoming the invasion of his tongue.

Christy went weak with need. She was melting from the heat. Burning up with fever. Consumed with a sweet warmth that threatened to devour her. "No," she whimpered. "We can't do...this."

Cody raised his hands and braced them against the sides of her face, holding her prisoner. "Yes," he murmured against her lips, "we can. We will."

Cody was going too fast for her. Oh, sweet heaven, her own body was going too fast for her. She felt as though she were sitting atop a runaway horse, galloping out of control, being propelled farther and farther away from sound reason.

"I feel as if I've been waiting all my life for you," Cody whispered, wrapping his arms completely around her. His hand reached up to smooth the hair from her temple, his touch gentle and concerned. "I can only imagine what you think of me coming here like this."

Her eyes remained closed, and her dark world continued to spin out of control. Even when she focused her eyes open, everything was blurred and out of focus, her thoughts hopelessly addled.

"I didn't mean to shock you."

"You didn't. I shocked myself."

Cody sensuously worked his thumbs across the high curve of her cheekbones. He frowned as he felt the moisture, and paused, his face tightening with concern. "I hurt you?"

"No..." she murmured, looking away. Now she understood the restless, brooding feeling she'd experienced all night. She'd been haunted by his kiss, haunted by the emotions and need he'd created within her.

All this had to stop. Now. This instant. She pressed her forehead against his solid chest, needing his strength in order to gain the courage to say what she must.

His hand found her hair, lifting the tresses, his touch gentle as though fingering delicate strands of silk.

"I fall apart when you kiss me," she confessed.

His throaty laugh was filled with amusement and tenderness. "You fall apart?" He captured her hand and pressed it over his heart. "See what you do to me?"

She didn't need to touch him to realize his pulse was churning like a giant oil drill beneath her palm. Unable to watch the disillusionment in his eyes when she told him about James, she closed her own.

"I've never felt anything for anyone as strongly as I have for you," she stated softly. Then she didn't say anything more for a long moment, carefully formulating her words.

Cody must have sensed that something was troubling her because he tucked his finger under her chin and raised her head. His gaze caressed her. "Christy?"

"Please listen," she whispered, her voice trembling. "There's something you should know, something I meant to tell you from the first, only..."

"Cody, what are you doing here?" Russ's voice echoed through the barn like thunder. "Everything's all right with Taylor, isn't it?" Christy's brother-in-law stopped short when he found Cody's arms wrapped around her waist. He removed his Stetson and wiped his forearm over his brow. "I wasn't interrupting anything, was I?"

"Your timing couldn't be worse," Cody barked, glaring at his friend.

Russ didn't appear the least bit threatened. He tossed a load of baling wire into the back of his pickup and promptly reached for another. If anything, he looked downright amused.

"That isn't funny."

Russ paused. "Now that's the part where I disagree. You only just met Christy. Until yesterday you hadn't so much as set eyes on her. I don't mind telling you, Cody Franklin, I've never known you to work so fast."

"Shut your fool mouth before you say something I'll make you regret," Cody grumbled. His threat wasn't worth a dime and Russ knew it, but he felt he had to say something.

"She is a pretty little thing, isn't she?" Another wheel of wire landed on top of the first with a loud, discordant clang. He paused and turned to stare at Cody when he didn't answer right away. "Isn't she?" he repeated.

"Yes," Cody admitted grudgingly.

"For a moment there it looked like the two of you had been kissing." Once more Russ paused, a grin turning the edges of his mouth.

"I *was* kissing her," Cody said in such a way to challenge Russ to make something of the fact if he wanted to. He was as uncomfortable as he could ever remember being with his friend. Russ was curious as hell to find out what was going on between him and Christy. Unfortunately Cody could think of no way of explaining his feelings for Christy, especially in the mood Russ was in. His friend seemed to find the situation downright comical.

"I guessed as much." Once more Russ wiped the sweat from his brow, but Cody had a sneaking suspicion that he did so in an effort to cover a smile. Not that Russ had any trouble poking fun at him.

Russ had arrived, and the three of them had exchanged pleasantries before Christy excused herself and left, explaining that she was driving to Miles City to visit Taylor and Eric. Cody would have offered to go with her, but he was working swing shift and it wasn't likely that he'd be back before he was scheduled to go on duty.

"You're not going to get closemouthed with me now, are you?" Russ asked. "I can't say I remember you ever taking to a woman the way you have to Taylor's sister. What's different about Christy?"

"What was different about Taylor?"

Russ chuckled. "Touché. But if you remember correctly, all Taylor and I could do was argue. Never met a woman who could irritate me as much as she did."

"You didn't stay angry at her for long."

Russ chuckled. "No, I can't say that I did. She'd make me so furious I couldn't think straight. Before I could stop myself, I'd say or do some fool thing I'd end up regretting. That certainly doesn't seem to be the case with you and Christy, though. You two can't seem to keep your hands off each other."

Cody decided it was best to ignore that comment. "You and Taylor worked things out, and that's what matters."

Some of the humor drained from Russ's dark eyes. "We did, didn't we?" He hesitated, and a faraway look came over him. "Did you get a good look at him, Cody?"

Before Cody could respond Russ continued. "The nurse handed me Eric, and I swear something happened to my heart. It was the craziest thing, holding that baby in my arms and loving him so much my throat got all clogged up. I couldn't have said a word if my life had depended on it. Before I knew what was happening, tears were rolling down my face. Me, man. I can't remember the last time I cried. I don't recall ever feeling anything as incredible as holding my son.

"I thought I loved Taylor before the baby was born, but it pales by what I felt for her as she struggled to give birth to Eric. You know, I've always thought of women as the weaker sex, but I've been wrong all along." He shook himself as if waking from a deep sleep. His friend's eyes were as serious as Cody had ever seen them.

"You have reason to be proud."

"I bought every box of cigars the gift shop owned."

"I know. I was with you."

"Hell, I don't even smoke."

Cody chuckled. "I know that, too." He hesitated, uncertain how to proceed. "About Christy... You don't have any objection to my seeing her, do you?"

"So you plan to take her to Sitting Bull Lookout?" The ridge that looked out over the city had been their favorite necking place as teenagers.

"Probably," Cody answered, struggling to hold back a grin.

Russ tucked his hands into his hip pockets. "Then you really are serious?"

"I've never been more serious in my life," Cody admitted without a pause.

Taylor was sound asleep when Christy arrived at the hospital. Her sister was lying back on the pillows, her long, thick hair spread out like spilled coffee, her eyes closed, her breathing deep and even.

Tiptoeing into the room so as not to disturb her, Christy pulled out the lone chair and sat. Although she'd been on the road more than an hour, she remained as upset and nervous as when she'd left the house.

She felt like weeping. She felt like rejoicing. No woman should experience such conflicting emotions. It was as if there were a giant tug-of-war being waged inside her.

The obedient, do-what's-right-at-all-costs part of her kept reminding her of James. Loyal, hardworking James, who loved her.

All her life Christy had done what was right. She'd never been rebellious. She'd been a model child. A model sister. A model's model. Respectful. Considerate. Thoughtful.

She felt none of those things now.

The look Cody had given her just before Russ stepped into the barn and interrupted them would be forever burned in her mind. It was the type of look a woman dreams a man will grant her sometime in her life. A lover's look. One so intimate and personal that it could never be explained to another.

If this incredible feeling between her and Cody was so wrong, then why did Christy feel so good inside? Why did she long to throw up her arms and shout for joy? If this was being rebellious or disrespectful, then all Christy could say was that she was entering her puberty later than the normal teenager. About ten years later.

Taylor stirred and opened her eyes. "Christy," she said, yawning. "When did you arrive?"

"About five minutes ago."

"You should have woken me."

"And interrupt your nap?" she teased. "How are you feeling?"

"Incredible. Wonderful." A soft smile touched her eyes. "Eric spent most of the morning with me. Oh, Christy, he's so adorable. We became acquainted with each other. I counted his fingers and toes, and he taught me a thing or two about breast feeding."

"You look happy."

"I am . . . I really am."

Christy settled farther down in the chair. Trying not to be obvious, she cast her gaze on the floor, studying the pattern of the white tile. "Cody took me out to eat when we left here yesterday."

"Here in Miles City?"

"No. We went to the bowling alley in Cougar Point."

"He's a good man."

Christy knew that instinctively. "I thought so, too. I like him, Taylor. I really do."

"Why do you look so guilty about it?"

How could she look or feel anything else? Only Taylor wouldn't understand. Her sister had no way of knowing about the lovely solitaire being sized at the Seattle jewelers.

They chatted for a few minutes more before Taylor settled back against the thick pillows and sighed.

"What was that all about?"

"What?"

"That sigh," Christy said.

"Oh . . . I was just thinking about you and Cody. I'm really pleased you like him so much. Frankly I've been concerned about you seeing so much of James."

It was something of a minor miracle that Christy didn't give everything away. "Oh?" she managed.

"He's nice, don't get me wrong, but he's so dreadfully boring. To be honest, I've never understood what you saw in him."

"But he's kind."

"So is Big Bird!" Taylor argued. "I think James is a nice guy, but he isn't the right one for you, and frankly I can't understand why you continue to date him."

"How can you say that?" Christy demanded, forcing the argument. James had been a child prodigy, a recognized genius by age ten. He graduated from high school in his early teens, and from law school at twenty. At twenty-five he was close to becoming the youngest partner in Atwater and Beckham's long, distinguished history. "James is a wonderful man."

"True," Taylor agreed readily enough. "Only he isn't the right one for you."

"You're wrong." A simple end to this argument would be for Christy to announce her engagement to the attorney, yet she hesitated, interested in hearing her sister's opinion.

"James is everything you say, I agree, but you're not in love with him and never have been," Taylor announced with a soft, taunting smile.

"You sound so confident."

"I am. You couldn't possibly be in love with James if you're this interested in Cody Franklin."

Any argument Christy had been about to pose died a quick and quiet death.

"I think," Taylor said, holding out her hands to her sister, "you came to Montana at exactly the right time."

Chapter Four

"Can I hold Eric?" Mandy Palmer requested minutes after Taylor was home from the hospital. "I barely got the chance to look at him before," she added, casting an accusing glance in the direction of her older brother.

"Of course," Taylor said, leading the teenager into the living room. Russ followed, leaving Christy standing alone in the kitchen with Cody.

She busied herself at the stove, praying the sheriff would follow the others.

He didn't.

"You've been avoiding me," he said softly, leaning against the kitchen counter and crossing his arms over his powerful chest. It was all Christy could do not to stare at him. If she did, he was sure to read the longing in her eyes, sure to realize she'd been miserable and unhappy and at odds with herself.

She'd needed these two days to think. To come to grips with herself. To decide.

The answers hadn't come easily. She'd wrestled with herself, toiled with the most momentous decision of her life. The resolution had come, but not without a price. She felt drained, frightened and incredibly weak.

She couldn't deny Cody's words. She had been artfully avoiding him. She'd surprised herself at how clever she'd been. Imaginative enough that no one would have guessed.

Except Cody.

"Why didn't you answer my calls?" he demanded softly, insistently.

"I came to spend time with Taylor, to help her. I've been busy...."

No one had bothered to tell her Cody had been invited to Taylor and Eric's welcome home dinner. She wasn't prepared for this.

From the way everyone had disappeared the minute Taylor arrived, Christy shouldn't be surprised to find herself alone with Cody. It seemed as if it had all been prearranged.

"Christy, talk to me," he pleaded, his frustration evident. "Tell me what's wrong."

"Nothing, really. It's just that I've been so terribly busy." So terribly confused. So terribly guilty. Cowardly, too, since she was tossing around the truth, juggling with her conscience, her scruples and her sense of fair play.

If anything, this time away from Cody had enlightened her. The first day she'd been trapped in the restless, lost sensation she'd experienced the first night he'd left her. Both returned unexpectedly in full force. The vague uneasiness had plagued her more powerfully than ever.

The second day, however, she'd found peace. It was a strained peace and would continue to be so until she returned to Seattle. Nevertheless, she'd reached an armistice with herself.

For a good portion of the afternoon Mandy and Christy had worked together to get the house ready for Taylor's return with Eric. No one had bothered to mention Cody would be returning with them.

No one had given her a word of warning. She didn't know what to say to him, and the truth seemed unwieldy. Especially now that it contained a postscript.

"I don't blame you if you're frightened," Cody continued, his voice low and thoughtful. "I'm frightened myself. The first time we kissed I felt like I'd been hit by a freight train. The second time the sensation was even more powerful.... Deep down I'd hoped, believed, it was somehow tied up in the emotion surrounding Russ, Taylor and the baby, but it isn't."

"I don't think it is, either."

"If you're looking for an explanation of what's going on with us, I can't give you one. All I know is what I feel."

Sometimes, Christy believed, a lifetime of doing the right thing was held captive to sensation. This had certainly proved true with her and Cody.

"Talk to me."

Slowly she turned, witnessing for herself the tenderness, and the confusion, in his eyes. Without uttering a word, she walked over to him and slipped her arms around his waist. He wrapped his own around her, anchoring her to his chest as he expelled a harsh breath.

"Can you tell me what's troubling you?"

She nodded, almost giddy with relief and release. Raising her head, she smiled up at him, longing to reassure him. Part of her yearned to put this behind them and blurt it all out. She wanted to tell him everything about James and the engagement and how meeting him had tossed her world on its tail. But there wasn't enough time to fully untangle this mess now before dinner. They needed privacy to discuss this in detail, time to reach an understanding.

She glanced regretfully toward the living room.

"Do you want to steal away?" Cody asked.

That was exactly what she did want, but they couldn't leave. Tonight was an evening to celebrate. Taylor and Eric were home for the first time, and leaving would be selfish and thoughtless.

"Forget I asked that," Cody murmured. "I'll be patient."

"So will I. We'll make some excuse after dinner," she suggested, then on impulse reached up and lightly brushed her lips over his.

Cody, however, wanted more. Much more.

Placing his hands on each side of her neck, he pulled her tighter to him and wove his fingers through her short hair as he angled his mouth over hers.

He flirted with the seam of her lips and eased his tongue over her moist mouth. Once again Christy felt her legs began to melt like wax set too close to a fire. The tip of her tongue met his. They touched, they stroked, they played with each other until Christy was convinced she was about to faint.

"I swear," Russ claimed loudly, walking into the kitchen, "I can't leave these two alone for a moment." The words were followed by the sound of his amusement.

Languidly Cody eased his mouth from Christy's and slowly, ruefully, opened his eyes. "How about getting lost for the next couple of minutes?" Cody whispered.

"It's fine with me," Russ agreed, "but I don't think that fried chicken's going to want to wait much longer."

"Oh, my," Christy said, abruptly breaking away. She'd completely forgotten about the dinner she and Mandy had so carefully planned. She reached for a pot holder and moved the grease-spitting skillet from the burner. Heaving a sigh of relief, she brushed her bangs off her forehead.

"Do you need any help?" Mandy asked, sauntering into the kitchen. Russ's teenage sister lived with him and Taylor, and from everything Christy had heard, Mandy was the one responsible for bringing Russ and Taylor together. Because of school and other commitments, Mandy had been away from the house during most of Christy's visit and Christy was only beginning to get to know her. And like her.

"No. I've got everything under control here."

Russ contradicted her under his breath, but Christy chose to ignore her brother-in-law's comment. She was relieved when the two men vacated the kitchen.

With Mandy's assistance, dinner was ready fifteen minutes later. Mandy called everyone, and they gathered around the dining room table. Russ escorted his wife, his eyes tender as he seated her.

Taylor, wearing a loose pale blue dress that complemented her eye color, looked wonderful. Every woman should look so good three days after giving birth, Christy mused.

"Oh, Christy...Mandy," Taylor said, looking over the table. "This is fantastic. You must have spent the whole day cooking—and in this heat!"

"It wasn't a problem," Christy said automatically.

"Yes, it was," Mandy countered smoothly. "It took all afternoon, but we had so much fun it was worth it. Your sister's great!"

"I think so, too, but you two shouldn't have gone to so much trouble," Taylor whispered, glancing over the three different kinds of salads, the platter of fried chicken and two separate desserts.

"But we did," Mandy said, reaching for the potato salad, "so you might as well enjoy it."

Christy shared a secret smile with her older sister. She admired Mandy for her openness and her honesty. Had she answered, she would have quickly allowed Taylor and the others to believe she'd managed to whip up a three-course meal in a matter of minutes without the least bit of trouble.

Eric stirred just as they were finishing dinner, and Taylor immediately started to rise. Russ placed his hand on her arm, stopping her.

"Let me?" He made it a question.

"He probably needs his diaper changed," Taylor warned.

"So? I can do it. Just how difficult can changing a diaper be?"

Christy and Taylor exchanged a meaningful look. When she pulled her gaze away from her sister, Christy's eyes sought out Cody. The sheriff looked downright flabbergasted.

"Did I hear correctly?" he teased. "Did Russ Palmer just volunteer to change a diaper?"

"I think so," Taylor said, pretending to be as awed as Cody.

"All right, you guys, cut it out," Russ warned, shouting from inside the master bedroom.

"I don't know if I can let a moment like this pass without witnessing it myself. Does anyone have a camera?"

"You're not taking any damn picture," Russ roared, his voice booming through the house like thunder. His words were quickly followed by a squalling cry of an infant. A fraction of a second later Russ shouted for Taylor.

Christy tossed her napkin aside and left the table with her sister, wondering if she could help. Mandy was the only one content to let the others deal with the baby while she finished her meal. Christy was convinced the girl possessed a wisdom beyond her fifteen years.

The three of them were crowded around the bassinet while Russ struggled with the diaper and the pins. He was grumbling, and his face was creased with a deep frown as if he were performing surgery.

"I marry the most modern woman in the world. She won't let me open a car door for her, insists on paying for her own dinner when we got out on a date, but will she use disposable diapers? Oh, no, she's got to torment me with cloth ones."

"They're better for the environment," Taylor said, gently pushing her husband aside. She dealt efficiently with the diaper changing task as if she'd been doing it for a good portion of her life.

"That's all there is to it?" Cody asked, making fun of his friend's inability to handle the uncomplicated situation.

"If you think it's so easy, you try it."

"I will, but probably not for several years." Cody looked at Christy, and the mental image of Cody holding a baby in his arms, their baby, filled her mind. The image wrapped tight cords around her heart, and she looked away, not wanting anyone to witness the emotion she was feeling.

Russ watched as Taylor lifted the dirty diaper from the bassinet. "What are you going to do with that . . . thing?" He wrinkled his nose as he asked the question.

"I'm putting it in the diaper pail in the bathroom."

"You're not keeping those smelly diapers in there, are you?" he demanded as he followed Taylor down the narrow hallway. Christy could hear him listing his objections.

Once more Christy and Cody were left alone, this time with Eric. The infant lay on his back, squinting his blue eyes as he looked up at them. His small pink mouth made tiny sucking motions.

Unable to resist, Christy reached into the bassinet and lifted Eric. He gurgled contentedly in her arms as she sat on the end of the mattress. Cody stood next to her, studying the newborn. He reached down and lovingly smoothed his large hand along the side of the baby's head. Eric's tiny hand closed around Cody's index finger.

"Look," Cody said excitedly, as if Eric had broken an Olympic record. "I think he recognizes us."

"And well he should! We're his godparents," Christy reminded him. She turned to smile at Cody and once more found herself lost in his eyes.

Their gazes held, and in that brief moment Christy saw a reflection of everything she was feeling. Until now they'd look at each other, and their gazes would fill with questions and doubts, as if they needed a plausible explanation for this craziness that had engulfed them.

This time was different. Christy found in Cody an acceptance. An understanding. They each seemed to have lost the need for answers.

"How long will you be in Cougar Point?" Cody asked.

"My vacation is for two weeks."

Both seemed to take a moment to calculate the number of days remaining before she would need to return. Whatever it was seemed far too few.

Cody's look told her he wanted to spend every available moment he could with her. It was what Christy wanted, too, more than she'd wanted anything in a good long while.

"I'm working day shift tomorrow," he told her softly, his look tender. "What about dinner?"

"I'd like that." Which was something of an understatement.

The air between them seemed to spark with sensuality. Cody leaned toward her, and Christy knew beyond a doubt he intended to kiss her. He hesitated a fraction of an inch from her mouth before sighing and regretfully backing away.

"I'd bet my last dollar if I kissed you, Russ would interrupt us."

"He probably would. He seems to possess an incredible sense of timing, doesn't he?"

As soon as she spoke, her brother-in-law stuck his head in the doorway. "What's taking you two so long? Mandy's got the coffee poured."

"See what I mean?" Cody whispered.

Christy nodded and stood, gently placing Eric over her shoulder and rubbing his back. He was so incredibly tiny, so perfect, and her heart swelled anew with love for him.

Taylor and Russ were sitting in the living room when Cody and Christy appeared. Their looks were openly curious as if waiting for the couple to make an announcement.

Christy didn't think it would do much good to try to disguise what was going on between her and Cody. Her sister knew her far too well, and it was apparent Russ was equally familiar with Cody.

By tacit agreement, Christy and Cody sat at opposite sides of the room. Being close to each other only intensified the attraction, and no doubt the curiosity.

"So," Russ said, glancing from Cody to Christy, sporting a grin that would have made a Cheshire cat proud.

"Russ," Taylor warned in a low whisper.

"What?"

"Do you have to be so obvious?"

Russ blinked, apparently at a loss to understand his wife's censure. "I didn't say anything, but if I did venture to mention the obvious, I'd say something along the lines of how happy I am that my best friend and your sister have apparently hit it off so well."

"If the truth be known, I couldn't be more pleased with it myself," Taylor added, grinning.

Cody crossed his long legs and reached for his coffee. "I'm glad to hear Christy and I have made you two so happy."

Russ chuckled at that, the remnants of his amusement glistening in his eyes. "Do you remember that time in the sixth grade?" Russ asked, growing serious.

"I'm not likely to forget it."

"What are you two mumbling about now?" Taylor demanded.

"We were eleven."

"You were eleven," Cody corrected. "I was ten."

"Right," Russ admitted. "We'd been good friends for several years and had started to notice some of our other buddies turning traitor."

"Turning traitor?" Christy quizzed.

"Liking girls."

Since Christy was the youngest of the five Manning children, she couldn't remember her brothers sharing similar feelings. "I bet you wanted to line up all the girls in town and shoot them at dawn." She might not remember her brothers' attitude toward girls, but she was an expert in the art of teasing.

"Shooting them didn't occur to us," Russ said, "but it's a hell of a good idea. I'll pass it on to Eric in about ten or eleven years."

"What did you two do?" Taylor pressed.

"The only thing we could," Russ explained, grinning. "We were losing our best friends left and right, so Cody and I made a pact and became blood brothers. As I recall, we made a solemn vow never to associate with any of the guys who had turned traitor and had started to like girls."

"Especially pretty ones with dark hair and bright blue eyes," Cody remarked, looking at Christy, who possessed both. The edges of his mouth quivered, and she realized he was only a breath away from laughing outright.

"And which of you broke this sacred vow first?"

The men glared at each other. "Cody did," Russ claimed.

"Russ," Cody responded, the two speaking almost simultaneously.

"Boys, please," Taylor said in what Christy was sure was her best schoolteacher voice.

"Cody gave Mary Lu Hawkins a valentine that same year," Russ reminded him.

"My mother forced me to do it," Cody argued, as if pleading his case before a federal judge. "I never liked Mary Lu Hawkins, and you know it."

"That's not what I heard."

Listening to Cody and Russ was like witnessing an exchange between her own brothers. A strong sense of family was an integral part of who she was. She loved their frequent get-togethers and had missed Taylor dreadfully over the past year.

"Is it always like this between these two?" Christy asked her sister.

"It's sometimes worse," Taylor admitted out of the corner of her mouth.

"Russ was the ultimate traitor," Cody insisted, setting his coffee mug aside with a decisive action. "He married a dark-haired, blue-eyed woman, and worse, I wasn't even invited to the wedding."

"No one was," Mandy inserted as she stepped from the kitchen, drying her hands on her apron skirt. "Not even me. Russ's very own sister."

"I swear you're never going to forgive me for that, are you?" Russ grumbled, drawing in a deep breath as if he found the subject a painful one. "Just wait till you fall in love, little sister, then you might be more understanding."

Mandy straightened her spine and set back her shoulders. Her eyes narrowed as she glared across the room at her brother. The gesture reminded Christy so much of her older sister confronting their father that she nearly laughed out loud.

"It may come as a shock to you, big brother, but I've been in love several times." It was clear Mandy considered herself a woman of the world.

Russ made no bones about his opinions on that issue. He rolled his eyes.

"Russ," Taylor warned softly.

"Now what did I do?" he asked, clearly frustrated. At the rate he was going, his foot would remain a permanent part of his mouth. "All right, all right, I . . . we made a mistake by not having you attend the wedding ceremony. There. Are you satisfied?"

"No. I want you to admit that I'm old enough to be in love."

"Mandy!"

"Admit it." The teenager apparently had a will of iron and nerves of steel. It was clear brother and sister were often at odds, and yet Christy sensed the deep and abiding love they shared.

"Don't look at me, Russ Palmer," Taylor said bluntly. "You're the one who got yourself into this."

"I suppose that at fifteen a mature teenage girl may have experienced her first taste of love."

"May have?" Mandy repeated. "That's not good enough."

"My goodness, the girl wants blood."

"She's likely to get it, too," Taylor said, apparently for Christy's benefit.

"All right, I'll admit it. There! Now are you satisfied?"

Mandy smiled graciously and nodded. "Thank you, brother dearest."

"You're welcome, sister sweetest." But he didn't sound the least bit appreciative. He turned his attention away from Mandy. "Listen," Russ said, looking at

Cody and Christy and then back at his friend once more. His gaze grew intense. "If you two ever get married, whether it's to each other or anyone else, take some advice and don't do it in Reno."

"If Mandy was upset that she wasn't at the wedding, it was nothing compared to how strongly Mom and Dad felt about the issue," Taylor added. "Dad seemed to feel I'd cheated him out of an important part of fatherhood by not letting him escort me down the aisle."

From somewhere deep inside, Christy forced a smile. This talk about weddings was making her decidedly uncomfortable. What her sister said was true enough. Her parents had been bitterly disappointed not to hold a large wedding for their oldest daughter. It was one of the reasons they were so pleased when Christy announced she and James would be marrying. Almost immediately the elder Mannings had started talking about the large church ceremony, with a reception and dance following.

"I think it's time for us to go, don't you?" Cody said to Christy, unfolding his long legs and standing. He walked across the room in three long strides.

Christy stood and carefully handed Eric, who was sleeping soundly, to his mother.

"Where are you two headed?" Russ wanted to know, making no effort to disguise his interest.

"Out." Cody grinned at Christy, and his smile was like the warm fingers of sunlight in winter. They'd known each other such a short while, and it seemed inconceivable that she should feel so strongly for him. But she did. The reasons were no longer important. These feelings they shared were too complex to put into words.

"When will you be back?" Russ asked his sister-in-law, as if he wasn't completely convinced his best friend was safe in her company.

"Who appointed you my guardian angel?" Cody demanded, but was unable to disguise his amusement.

"I'm only looking out for your best interests," Russ explained, continuing the game. "Good grief, man, she's pretty with dark hair and blue eyes. We learned way back in the sixth grade those were the ones to watch out for. You've got to be careful. Look at what happened to me!"

"What did happen to you?" Taylor asked, her smooth brow wrinkling with the question.

"You should know. Before I even realized what was happening, I was saddled with a wife. I don't mind telling you, man, I'm worried for you."

"If I'm responsible for the security of an entire county then you can trust me to take care of myself."

"Saddled?" Taylor asked, her voice ominously low. "You found yourself *saddled* with a wife?"

Russ hedged, looking decidedly uncomfortable. "Maybe saddled wasn't the best word."

"Then I suggest you search for another."

"Ah..." Russ paused and rubbed his hand over the back of his neck several times.

"He's talking off the top of his head," Cody said, defending his longtime friend. He turned toward Russ. "If I were you, I'd plead for leniency and remind her how crazy in love you are with her."

"He dug himself into this hole. He can get himself out," Taylor warned.

"How about my being favored with a wife?" Russ suggested, glancing around the room. He looked downright pleased with his choice of the word.

Taylor glanced at Christy, a smile playing at the corners of her mouth, then abruptly shook her head. "That's not good enough."

"Taylor, come on, I'm having a serious discussion with my best friend here. All I'm looking to do is impart a few words of wisdom before Cody makes the same... before he ends up..."

"Ends up what?" Taylor prompted.

It took Russ several moments to answer. "Blessed?" he offered, confident he'd smoothed over any rough waters.

"Blessed is a good word."

"I think we should get out of here while the getting's good, don't you?" Cody asked, reaching for Christy's hand, entwining their fingers.

"I couldn't agree with you more." The solid ground beneath her feet seemed to shift as she realized that once they were alone she'd need to explain about James. Dragging in a steadying breath, she looked to Taylor. "I won't be gone long."

"If I get worried, I'll contact the sheriff," Taylor teased.

The phone rang, and Mandy shot out of the living room like a cannonball.

Russ escorted Christy and Cody to the back door.

Mandy appeared, stretching the long telephone cord into the kitchen. She looked confused as she held out the receiver to Russ. "I think it must be a wrong number. Maybe you should talk to him."

"All right."

Cody chuckled. "I never thought I'd be grateful for a phone call. I had the impression we were going to be forced to listen to more of Russ's pearls of wisdom."

They were all the way down the stairs when the back door swung open with enough force to send it crashing closed.

"Christy." Russ stood on the top of the steps, his hands on his hips, his eyes squinting against the setting sun.

"Yes?" She turned to face her brother-in-law. The humor had drained out of him, replaced instead with a fierce anger that transformed his handsome features.

Cody took a step forward. "What is it?"

"The phone," Russ said, glancing over her shoulder. "It's for Christy. Someone named James Wilkens."

She gasped softly before she could stop herself.

"He claims he's her fiancé."

Chapter Five

"Cody, please," Christy pleaded, her heart in her eyes. "I can explain."

"You mean it's true?" Russ shouted.

"It's not as bad as it sounds—if only you'd take the time to listen." Both of her hands gripped Cody's forearm as she boldly held on to him, not wanting to let him go for fear she'd never see him again.

"Are you engaged or not?" His dark eyes appeared as hot as molten rock, burning into hers, searing her conscience far deeper than any words he could have spoken.

"I was going to tell you about James...."

Cody's face tightened as though she'd delivered a crippling blow to his abdomen. He lowered his gaze to her hands, which were clenched tightly around his arm.

"I see." The two words sounded as though they'd been braided with brittle strands of steel.

She moistened her lips, unsure if she could trust her voice. "Please let me explain."

"What's there to say? It's a simple matter, isn't it? Either you're engaged or you're not." He pulled himself free and turned his back to her.

"Cody," she tried once more, hating the way her voice wobbled as she pleaded for patience and understanding.

One stern look told her he wasn't willing to grant her either. Her heart clenched painfully as she slowly dropped her hands and stepped away from him.

Without another word, Cody climbed inside his Cherokee, slammed the door and drove away as if the very demons of hell were in hot pursuit.

Christy went completely still. She couldn't move. Couldn't breathe. It was as if her feet had been planted in concrete blocks.

How long she stood there, Christy couldn't have said. Nor could she put order to her thoughts. Just a few moments ago she'd been sitting across the room from Cody, laughing with him, sharing secret smiles with him, her whole being permeated with a feeling of gladness and joy. How natural it had all seemed for them to be together. As natural as the sun setting. As natural as rain.

"Are you going to talk to your fiancé or not?" Russ demanded, his voice sharp with censure as he cut into her thoughts.

Christy stared at him for a moment or two before she realized James was still on the phone, waiting for her. Nevertheless, she stood as she was and watched the thick plume of dust that trailed behind Cody's vehicle. After a while it faded into the distance, taking with it the promise of something wonderful.

Russ waited for her at the top of the porch steps. Christy lowered her gaze as she stepped past him. He didn't need to say anything for her to feel his reprimand.

The telephone receiver was resting on a small table in the hallway. Christy stared at it for a moment, dragged in a deep, calming breath and reached for it. "Hello, James." She prayed her voice revealed none of her turmoil.

"Christy. How are you?" He sounded anxious, concerned.

"Fine, just fine. Taylor had the baby, but I suppose you've heard everything about that already. I doubt that Mom and Dad could keep quiet about Eric. He really is precious." She realized she was chattering but couldn't seem to make herself stop. "Montana is an incredible state. I haven't seen much of Cougar Point yet, except the bowling alley. I had breakfast there the other morning, only it was really the middle of the afternoon...the day Eric was born, actually."

"You ate breakfast at a bowling alley?"

"There's a restaurant there and the food is good—wonderful, in fact."

"How nice."

"How are you?" Christy felt obliged to ask, now that the billowing winds of her enthusiasm had collapsed like slack sails.

"Good. I miss you." He lowered his voice slightly as if he were admitting to something he shouldn't. "The office seems empty with you away."

James wasn't a man who was comfortable with sharing his emotions. Expressing affection was difficult. For him to phone and openly admit he missed her was akin to another man standing on a rooftop, throwing his arms open and shouting at the top of his voice that he was madly in love.

"I . . . I've been terribly busy."

"I was hoping you'd call me."

Disappointment echoed with each word. The statement was worse than a tongue-lashing.

"I'm sorry, James, really I am. It's just that everything happened so fast. I didn't even have a chance to unpack my bags before Taylor went into labor. She came home from the hospital today, and we . . . we were just having dinner." That was a slight exaggeration. They'd finished with their meal, but she needed an excuse to get off the phone before she did something stupid like weep uncontrollably, or tell him about Cody.

"You're having dinner? Dear heavens, why didn't you say something sooner? No wonder it took you so long to get to the phone."

Christy leaned her shoulder against the wall, closed her eyes and swallowed against the knot thickening in her throat. She felt strained by her minor deception, contaminated by the way she was deceiving him in an effort to cut short this painful conversation.

James deserved so much more than this. The guilt was crippling her, and it demanded all the self-control she possessed to keep from blurting out everything.

"I'll let you go, but before I do I want you to know that I got the diamond back from the jeweler. It'll be ready when you return from your sister's."

"H-how nice."

"Goodbye, Christy. Give my regards to Taylor and her husband and congratulate them both for me."

"I will. Goodbye, James. Don't work too hard."

"No, I won't."

She replaced the receiver. Her fingers curled around the handpiece in a death grip as she waited for the recriminations to rain down on her like huge hailstones. She needed something terrible to happen that would help her deal with this overwhelming sense of wrongdoing. Anything would be better than this horrible sense of remorse.

Raised voices came at her from inside the living room.

"The least you can do is listen to her." Christy heard Taylor shout.

"What possible explanation could she have? Either she's engaged or she isn't."

"Listen to me, Russ Palmer. I won't have you yelling at my sister. Whatever's happening between her and Cody is her business. It doesn't have anything to do with us."

"Like hell I'm going to stay out of it. We're talking about Cody here—my best friend. I thought he was your friend, too."

"He is."

"Then you can't honestly expect to sit idly by and watch him get hurt, do you?"

"Please," Christy said, stepping into the room. She couldn't bear to have them argue over her. "Please...don't fight."

The room went silent. The quiet was so profound, it seemed to throb like a giant heart. Taylor's gaze locked with Christy's, clouded with doubt and uncertainty. Russ's eyes were filled with reproach.

Silence. Doubt. Reproach. All three filled the room like tangible entities. Christy felt them slam against her with the force of giant waves.

Russ and Taylor continued to stare at her. Russ was angry and made no effort to disguise his feelings. Taylor, usually so strong and confident, couldn't hide her confusion.

Christy suspected her sister was as troubled as her husband. Only Taylor wouldn't allow herself to voice her misgivings because of family loyalty.

"Sit down," Taylor suggested. She motioned toward the recliner where Christy had sat earlier. "You're so pale. Are you sure you're all right?"

"Why didn't you tell us you were engaged?" Russ demanded, barely giving her time to compose herself. "And if you and James are planning to marry, why the hell aren't you wearing a ring?"

"Russ, please," Taylor pleaded, "give her a chance to answer one question before hitting her with another." Directing her attention to Christy, Taylor's eyes rounded. "We're waiting."

Folding her hands together in her lap, Christy squeezed her fingers so tightly that they began to lose feeling. "James asked me to marry him two days before I left Seattle."

"He didn't offer you an engagement ring?"

"Of course . . . it's being sized now."

"I see," Taylor said, frowning. "And you didn't mention it to anyone? Do Mom and Dad know? I'm your sister, for heaven's sake. The least you might have done is mention the fact to me."

"Taylor," Russ said gruffly, then reminded her of her own words. "Give her a chance. She can only answer one question at a time."

"There wasn't time to tell you when I first arrived. Remember? Then first thing the next morning you went into labor and . . . I met Cody."

"You had no business leading him on," Russ snapped.

"I didn't mean to," she cried, and raked her fingers though her short hair, praying Taylor and Russ wouldn't condemn her. "It just . . . happened. We were both so excited about the baby and went out to eat to celebrate. Then Cody drove me home and . . . and I knew he was going to kiss me. I realize it was a mistake not to have said anything to him, but I was afraid . . ." Afraid that if she had said something he wouldn't have touched her, and she'd wanted his kiss so much.

Unable to meet her sister's eyes, she glanced down at the coffee table as the tears filled her eyes.

"Who the hell is this James character, anyway?" Russ asked Taylor. "Did we meet him?"

She nodded. "He's the attorney Christy introduced to us last summer."

"Not the . . ." He hesitated.

"Why didn't you tell me?" Taylor apparently considered it a personal affront that Christy had kept the news to herself. "We had plenty of time to talk while I was in the hospital and you were there every day."

"I tried several times," she said in her defense. "But every time I mentioned James, you changed the subject. And when I was finally able to drag him back into the conversation, you started telling me how dry and boring you think he is and what a mismatched couple we are. What was I supposed to do? Tell you I'd agreed to marry the man you'd just finished criticizing?"

"Oh, dear," Taylor whispered. "Now that you mention it, I do remember you trying to bring James into the conversation."

"Fine. You two got that settled, but what about Cody?" Russ stalked to the other side of the room and stared out the front window. "I can't, I won't let this happen to him a second time. Not when it's in my power to put an end to it." Gradually he turned around, his shoulder square and his jaw tightly clenched.

"A second time?" Christy echoed.

When Russ didn't respond right away, she looked at her sister, who was busy with Eric. Either that or she was avoiding eye contact. "Taylor?"

"It happened several years ago now," Russ began grudgingly. "A woman by the name of Rebecca Morgan moved into town. She was from the South and had the sweetest, gentlest manners you can imagine. She was the type of woman a man thinks about when the time comes to fall in love. And Becca was perfect. Beautiful. Demure. Sweet as candy and..." Russ paused long enough to shake his head. "Who would have ever guessed?"

"Guessed what?" Christy asked.

"Becca made it obvious from the moment she moved into town that she was attracted to Cody. Every time he turned around she was there, batting her eyes at him, doing those things you women do to let a man know you're interested."

"I could make a comment here, but I won't," Taylor muttered.

"Soon Becca and Cody were seeing a lot of each other. You have to understand, Cody isn't one to have his head easily turned, especially by a pretty woman. Until recently." He frowned at Christy as he said it. "But Becca did more than interest him. For the first time in his life, Cody was in love. It showed in everything he said and did.

"Cody's always been popular with the folks around here, and his happiness seemed to rub off on everyone.

Most folks liked Becca, too. They couldn't help themselves. There was plenty of talk of the two of them marrying." Russ paused long enough to walk over to the ottoman and sit down. "About a month after she moved into town a series of baffling robberies started happening."

"You don't mean to say Becca..."

"Not her personally. She was part of a team. Part of a scam that worked small cities all across the western states. Apparently the heat was on in several of the larger cities, and she and her partner decided to try their hand in small towns. They were damn successful, too. Becca would move into a town and get involved with a deputy from the local sheriff's office. One way or another she would get what information she could about shipments of money. Then she'd relay the information to her partner. It was all cleverly done. Whenever a shipment of cash was due to arrive, Becca would throw up a smoke screen. Two banks were robbed, and a couple of stores lost valuable equipment all within the second month she was in town. No one would suspect her. How could they? She was as gentle as a lamb and as sweet as honey."

"How long did it take Cody to realize it was Becca?"

"Not long, a few weeks, but you'll never convince him of that. He felt like the biggest fool who ever lived. He took responsibility for everything, blamed himself for not picking up on the scam sooner."

"But he loved her. Trusted her."

Russ's dark gaze collided with Christy's. "I know. He personally arrested her and her partner and testified against them in a court of law."

"Surely no one blamed Cody."

"No, everyone in town was as taken by her as he was. Cody wasn't the only one, but he felt as responsible as if he'd personally handed over the money. It's his job to protect and to serve and he felt he'd let the entire county down, although God knows he worked his fool head off until every penny taken was returned. Even that wasn't enough. Cody felt he had to resign from the department."

"No." Christy's response was immediate. True, she'd only known Cody a short while, but even in that time she'd learned how important law enforcement was to him. It was part of his heritage.

"Thankfully some of us were able to talk some sense into him. He made the mistake of falling in love with the wrong woman, but then again, it was all due to his efforts that Becca and her friend were caught. If it hadn't been for Cody, no one knows how long their little scam would have worked or how many other communities would have been bilked. Unfortunately Cody didn't see it that way."

"He was only human." Christy felt a burning need to defend him.

"Becca used him. But worse than that, she made him feel like a fool. It's taken three long years for him to live it down, at least in his own mind. The way most folks figured it, Cody had done Montana a good deed by putting Becca and her partner behind bars."

"Then that's why he wouldn't run for sheriff until last year?" Taylor asked.

"It's been his life's dream to be elected sheriff of Custer County, but it's taken all this time for him to agree to run. I suppose he felt he had to prove his worth all over again. The crazy part of all this is that he could have won hands down any year, including the one in which he was involved with Becca.''

"I didn't know," Taylor said softly.

"It's not something that's talked about a lot," Russ explained. "The subject is such a painful one, it's best forgotten."

"Then Becca's still in prison?" Christy managed to ask. Knowing how Cody had been deceived was painful for her, too. A sense of justice somehow made it easier to accept.

"From what I understand, she's tried to contact Cody a couple of times, claiming she really was in love with him, and still is. To hear her tell it, she was a helpless pawn in all this. She says she was a victim of blackmail. But Cody won't have anything to do with her.''

"I don't blame him." Taylor gently rubbed Eric's tiny back as she spoke.

"You aren't comparing me to Becca, are you?" Christy asked, feeling all the more wretched.

"You're no thief," Russ said abruptly. "I'm not worried about you bilking the good citizens of Cougar Point, if that's what you think. No..." He paused and rubbed his hand along the back of his neck. "After Becca something changed in Cody. He rarely dated. He closed himself off, became more pensive, intense. It was as if he'd lost trust in all women.''

Taylor nodded. "I can't say that I blame him."

"I don't, either," Christy added, realizing as she did so that she was condemning herself.

Russ frowned. "That's why I was so pleased at what happened after he met you. He would look at you, and it was like seeing the old Cody all over again, the man who smiled frequently, the man who joked freely. I don't know what went on between you." He hesitated and glanced to his wife. "Taylor's right when she says it isn't any of my business, but I won't stand by and let you take advantage of him."

"I wouldn't . . . I couldn't."

"Then why the hell didn't you tell him you were engaged?"

Christy felt as if she'd been backed into a corner. "I planned to. I never intended to keep it a secret, but I had to have time to think everything out. You may not believe this, but I'd hoped to talk to Cody tonight about James. I was going to tell him everything."

"Are you planning on marrying James?" Taylor asked, her eyes seeking out Christy's.

The question came as something of a shock. "No. I couldn't—not after meeting Cody."

"Then why the hell didn't you break the engagement when you had the chance?" Russ demanded. "You were just talking to him. It would have been a simple matter to be done with it."

"I can't do it over the phone," Christy said, and jerked her head upward. "James is a good man. He deserves better than that. He hasn't done anything wrong, and he really is a good person. I hate to hurt him. . . ." She paused when hot tears threatened to spill down her face. Biting her lower lip, she drew in a rickety breath.

"Christy's right." Taylor's words cut through the emotion-packed moment. "This is a delicate situation. You can't expect her to call James and break off the engagement. That would be heartless. This is something best done in person. James may be a tad bit dull, but he is a decent human being."

"Is . . . is there any chance Cody will talk to me?" It was in Christy's mind to drive into town and explain she had no intention of returning to Seattle and going through with the marriage. She couldn't do that, not now. Not after meeting Cody.

"I doubt he'll have anything to do with you," Russ answered, confirming her worst fears.

"Wait until tomorrow," Taylor advised. "Give him the space to think matters through."

"He asked me out to dinner.... But I don't know if he'll show or not."

"He won't," Russ interjected without pause. "I know him better than anyone, and I can tell you, as far as he's concerned, whatever was between you is over."

Christy's shoulders sagged with abject defeat. "I was afraid of that."

"Don't make it sound so hopeless," Taylor said.

"She's engaged, for God's sake. What do you expect him to do?" Russ shouted. "Ignore the fact? Cody isn't going to do that."

"But I have every intention of breaking off the engagement."

"I doubt that'll make any difference to him. I'd be surprised if he even took the time to listen to you."

"That's not true," Taylor countered confidently. "Cody's a reasonable man, and it's apparent he's attracted to you."

"He isn't anymore," Russ grumbled.

Taylor shot daggers at her husband. "Russ Palmer, kindly allow me to finish."

"Feel free, but you've got to understand. After Becca, Cody doesn't have a whole lot of trust in the opposite sex."

"Who can blame him after what Becca did?" Christy inserted.

Russ nodded. "Never again will he let another woman use him."

"My sister isn't another Becca."

"You and I know that."

A short silence followed before Christy said, "Cody's smart enough to know it, too." She wanted to believe it. Needed to believe it. But whether that was the case or not was something she would soon discover.

Cody slammed his fist against the steering column of the four-wheel-drive vehicle. He was parked on the ridge that overlooked Cougar Point and had been sitting there for the past hour, collecting his thoughts.

Frustration and anger mounted with each passing minute. Drawing in a deep breath, he rubbed his hands down his face, confident he'd been within a hairbreadth of making a world-class fool of himself for the second time.

When was he going to learn? Women weren't to be trusted. Especially pretty blue-eyed ones who looked as pure as freshly fallen snow. On the outside they were all sweetness, but inside... His thoughts skidded to an abrupt halt despite his best efforts to think badly of Christy.

He couldn't force himself to compare Becca with Taylor's sister. The two women shared little, if anything, in common. Becca was a con artist. Christy wouldn't know how to deceive anyone.

But she had.

She'd deceived him.

Once more he rubbed his hand down his face. Had she really? Hadn't she claimed there was something she needed to tell him? He'd stood in Russ's kitchen, looked into her beautiful eyes and had seen for himself the turmoil churning inside her. He'd been unable to understand, unable to grasp what was troubling her.

But right now all Cody could think about was himself. For the first time in years he'd been able to feel again. For the first time in years he'd been whole.

The sensation of wholeness hadn't gone completely away, although he suspected it would in time. The only thing he was experiencing currently was an ache that cut far deeper than anything he'd known in a good long while. What he felt for Christy had been a cruel joke.

"You don't honestly expect Cody's going to come, do you?" Taylor asked as Christy sprayed her carefully styled hair. She'd spent the past half hour fussing with her makeup and hair, hoping if she looked her best, it would lend her confidence.

"No. But I want to be ready in case he does."

"You've been restless all day," her sister accused softly.

"I know. I can't help it. Oh, Taylor, I can't bear to let things end this way between Cody and me. Everything felt so incredibly right with us."

"It's hard, isn't it?"

She nodded, battling down the need to rush to him and make him understand. "His eyes were so cold. I didn't know anyone could look so..." She couldn't think of a word strong enough to explain her fears.

For a good portion of the night she'd wrestled with the sheets and blankets in an effort to find a comfortable position. Once she did get cozy and closed her eyes, the disdainful look on Cody's face would pop into her mind. Her eyes would fly open, and the need to explain would dominate her thoughts.

She'd spent most of the night composing what she was going to say. All day she'd been mentally rehearsing so when the time came she'd be ready.

But she didn't feel ready now. She felt uneasy and scared, as if nothing she could say or do would make a difference.

"If he doesn't come to pick you up, what do you plan to do?"

"Go to him," Christy said firmly. "He made a date, and he's going to keep it whether he wants to or not."

A quick smile flashed from Taylor's eyes, and her lips quivered with the effort to suppress it. "I see."

"I mean it. If Cody isn't man enough to give me a chance to explain, then he deserved what he's going to get."

"And what's that?"

"I haven't got that figured out yet, but I'll think of something."

"Yes, I suppose you will," Taylor said on her way out of the bathroom.

Once she was finished, Christy joined her sister, who was busy with the dinner preparations. "Let me help," she insisted, feeling slightly guilty that Taylor would be stuck with the cooking. The very reason Christy was in Montana was to help with the household chores while Taylor recuperated.

"Don't be silly. I'm perfectly fine. Besides, you might do something to mess your makeup." Leaning her hip against the counter, Taylor did an extended survey of Christy's attire. "Personally I don't think Cody's going to be able to take his eyes off you."

"Oh, Taylor, do you really think so?" Looking her best was important to Christy. If Cody was going to slam the door in her face, which was a distinct possibility, then she wanted him to know what he was missing.

"There's something different about you," Taylor went on to say, her expression somber. She crossed her arms and cocked her head to one side as she composed her thoughts.

"You mean the eyeliner. I'm using a different shade."

"No, this doesn't have anything to do with eyeliner. You're not the same Christy I left when I moved away from Seattle."

"I'm older," Christy offered, "and hopefully more mature."

Taylor paused to consider that. "I suppose that's part of it, but there's something more."

"Oh?"

"You were always the 'good daughter.'"

"You make it sound like you were the bad one, and that isn't the least bit true."

"But we both know I love an argument," Taylor went on, "and Dad was willing enough to comply. We were so often at odds."

"But you and Dad always loved and respected each other. It wasn't like some families."

"I know. It's just that we're so different. About the worst thing I can ever remember you doing was running around the house with a pair of scissors in your hand."

"I did go swimming that one time without a bathing cap in the community pool, remember?"

"Ah, yes, I'd forgotten about that. You renegade!"

They laughed. What Taylor was saying was true. Christy had never caused a problem, never been in trouble. The good child. The good daughter. The good student. Too good, in some ways.

"You realize Mom and Dad are going to be disappointed when they learn you aren't going to marry James."

"Probably more disappointed than James," Christy joked.

Taylor frowned slightly. "Are you sure you're doing the right thing?"

The question was unexpected. "Of course. Soon after I met Cody, I realized I should never have agreed to marry James. I..."

"Then why did you?"

"Well...because we're friends and we'd been working a lot of hours together, and at the time it seemed the right thing to do."

"Your decision had nothing to do with Mom and Dad?"

"I...ah..."

"I don't mean to pressure you, or sound like a know-it-all, but if you check your motives, I think you might discover you accepted James's proposal for all the wrong reasons. It suited Mom and Dad for you to marry him, and you went along with it because you were looking to please them. Am I right?"

"I..." Christy lowered her gaze as a tingling feeling extended from her stomach to her arms and down her fingers. She loved her parents so much and wanted to make them proud of her. Her marrying James would certainly have done that. Christy had been so concerned about doing what her parents thought was right that she'd never considered if it was best for her.

"Christy?"

"You make me sound so weak, so insecure."

"You're not. You're loving and gentle and good. James is a fine young man, but he's not the one for you."

Without question her parents would be upset with her, but in time they'd realize she was doing what was best for both her and James.

Christy left the Lazy P soon afterward, not bothering to wait to see if Cody was going to come for her or not. It was clear from the way he'd left the evening before that he had no intention of keeping their dinner date.

She found his address without a problem and parked her car. She took several moments to compose herself before making her way to the front door.

An eternity passed before he answered her knock. "Christy?"

"I believe we have a dinner date," she said boldly, damning her voice for shaking the way it did. She didn't want him to guess how terribly nervous confronting him made her.

"A dinner date? You and me? No way, sweetheart. If you want to go out, call your fiancé."

Chapter Six

"I'm not going to marry James," Christy explained in a voice that demanded Cody listen to her and at the same time begged for his understanding. Cody wasn't in the mood to respond to either. From the moment he'd left Christy the night before, he'd waged a battle to push every thought of her from his mind.

With damn little success.

"Who you marry or don't marry is none of my concern," he said, his words sharp and abrupt.

Christy flinched at the cutting edge of his disdain, and it was all Cody could do to keep from reaching for her and asking her forgiveness.

"Please, if only you'd give me a chance to explain."

Damn but she was beautiful, with her cobalt-blue eyes and her sweet, innocent face. Until he'd met Christy and Taylor, Cody had never seen eyes that precise shade of blue.

He groaned inwardly, battling against the need to take her in his arms and bask in her softness. Equally strong was the instinctive urge to protect his heart and his orderly life from the havoc she was sure to bring.

Cody was the sheriff-elect, but there was little that could terrify him the way this tiny slip of a woman did. It was essential to keep his eyes trained away from her. Everything about her was sensual and provocative. Already his body was hardening. It was demanding enough to fight her, but the battle was made more fierce as he struggled with his own desires. Damn it all, this was far more difficult than he ever imagined it would be.

"At least talk to me."

Her voice was soft and sweet, compelling and gentle. The mere sound of her was enough to drive him straight through the bounds of what was fast becoming his limited self-control.

"I think you should leave."

There, he'd said it. He didn't mean it, but he'd said it, and that little bit of resistance lent him a sense of control, which had been sadly lacking to this point. Christy wasn't aware of it, but he was.

"I'm not leaving until you've listened to me."

"Then you're going to have to do your talking from the street." It amazed him how forceful he sounded. His large frame blocked the doorway as he indolently leaned against the jamb, trying his best to appear as though he hadn't a care in the world.

She hesitated, then surprised him by nodding. "Fine. If that's what it takes, I'll shout at you from the middle of the damn street, loud enough for the entire block to hear."

"You're wasting your time." He'd played these games with another woman once before, and he wasn't about to fall into that trap a second time.

Feeling confident, perhaps overly so, he straightened, leaned forward and braced his hands against her shoulders, keeping her at arm's length. It was a risk to touch her, but one he was prepared to take. Perhaps he felt the necessity to convince himself he could be close to her and not feel compelled to kiss her.

His plan backfired the instant she looked directly up at him with her baby blues. To complicate matters, she flattened her hands over his chest. His heart reacted instantly, and he was certain she could feel the effect she had on him. Maybe touching her wasn't such a smart move, after all.

"I meant what I said." He narrowed his eyes, hoping she'd take the hint and leave. In the same breath he prayed she wouldn't. Talk about being ambivalent!

"You have every right to be angry," Christy continued, her eyes pleading with him. "I don't blame you. I intended to tell you about James and me. Remember when we were in the kitchen before dinner I told you there was something I needed to talk to you about?"

She didn't give him a chance to answer. Not that it mattered; he did remember, all too well.

"It was never my intention to mislead you. I would have explained everything except James phoned before I had the chance."

Cody felt himself weakening. This wasn't supposed to be happening. He should be a tower of strength. A bastion of fortitude. With little more than a shrug of his shoulders he ought to send her packing. One woman had mercilessly used him before. Only an idiot would willingly allow it to happen a second time.

"I realized the first time you kissed me that I could never marry James," she persisted softly. "Maybe even before then. I know it should have been a simple decision, but it wasn't. I had to take some time to think everything through. The answer was so obvious, so clear, but I found that understanding it frightened me terribly."

She was frightened! Hell, Cody was shaking in his boots!

He dropped his hands, freely admitting touching her had been a tactical error.

"So you've broken it off?" he asked, hating the way his heart reacted to the possibility she was free.

Christy dropped her gaze so fast it was a wonder she didn't strain the muscles at the back of her neck. "Not exactly. But I promise you I will the minute I get back to Seattle."

A flood of ice raced through Cody's blood. So she intended to string him along. At least she was being honest about it, but frankly that didn't account for much.

"I know it sounds bad," she pleaded softly. "You might think it'd be better for me to contact James now. I thought so myself at first, but then I realized that it wouldn't be right. James doesn't deserve to be treated so heartlessly. He's a good man—it would be wrong to call him and flippantly explain that I'd met someone else. It just seems unnecessarily cruel to do it over the phone."

Cody snorted a soft laugh. She was a candidate for the loony bin if she expected him to buy into that. Either she was engaged to James or she wasn't. Either the wedding was on or it was off. It was as simple as that.

Life didn't need to be this complicated.

"All right," she said, and he could see her fighting to hold on to her composure. "If you can't accept that, I'll phone James and talk to him right now."

"Fine." He led the way into the house and didn't stop until he reached the kitchen phone. Feeling slightly cocky, he lifted the receiver and handed it to her, fully expecting her not to go through with the call. She was putting on a brave front, but inwardly he knew she had no intention of following through.

She stared at the receiver for a moment before taking it out of his hand. When she did, Cody realized how deathly pale she'd gone. Her breathing was downright choppy.

She offered him a quick, reassuring smile. "You're right," she said weakly. "I shouldn't be thinking about James's feelings at a time like this. You have feelings, too. It's probably best to get this over with now. James is a good man. He'll understand. I know he will." As if her fingers weighed a thousand pounds, she lifted her hand and punched out a series of numbers, then closed her eyes as she waited. "I'm sure he's still at the office."

After what seemed like an inordinate amount of time, and a short conversation with the receptionist, Christy replaced the receiver. "James had already left. He's probably at home by now. I'll try there...only..." She looked up to him, her eyes wide and wrought with tension. She was willing to do this because Cody demanded it of her, but it was killing her on the inside.

"Only what?" he prompted.

"Could you kiss me? I seem to need it right now."

His mouth found hers even before she'd finished speaking. It was in his mind to brush his lips gently across hers. This wasn't the time for anything more.

Christy sighed. At least Cody assumed it was her sighing. Then again maybe he was the one making all the noise. To be on the safe side, he kissed her again—just to be sure. Just so he'd know for a fact that he could walk away from her in a blink of an eye.

That was Cody's second tactical error of the evening.

She tasted like heaven, all sweet and warm, and before he was sure how it happened, his kisses were hungry beyond reason. He captured her waist, dragging her against him until the soft peaks of her breasts were pressed against his chest. She wasn't supposed to feel this good in his arms. Nothing was supposed to feel this incredible.

His mouth continued to move over hers until her lips parted. She sighed deeply and sagged against him as his tongue swept her mouth. Her response to his kisses left no room for doubt or questions. Her tongue parried with his, mimicked his, stroking and surrendering.

Cody had been so long without a woman that he could feel the heat rise in him as if he were being consumed by a mighty fever. He was the flame, and she was the kindling. Each kiss, each movement of her soft body against his hardening one, stoked the fire. Higher. Hotter.

It was either break away from her that moment or take her right there on his kitchen floor, an idea that was gaining momentum with each passing second.

"Christy," he panted, dragging his mouth from hers. He held her away from him in an effort to interject cool reasoning where little was in evidence. "No more."

She didn't answer him but instead wrapped her arms around his middle and buried her face in the curve of his neck. Her breathing was as hard and as uneven as his own. His hands were splayed across her back, and he held on to her with what little strength he'd managed to reserve.

Holding her this close brought into focus how wonderfully different her body was from his. While she was warmth and softness, all curves and valleys, he was hard planes and deep ridges. His whole body felt as if it were throbbing, so loud and so strong that the sound of it roared in his ears.

"Give me a moment and I'll phone James at his house," she whispered, her voice raspy and warm against his neck.

Cody framed her oval face in his hands. "No," he whispered, shocked by how thick his voice was.

"No?"

"I'm not happy with the situation, but you're right. Breaking the engagement by phone would be insensitive. I can wait until you get back to Seattle and can talk to him face-to-face."

She lowered her dark blue eyes in gratitude, her thick lashes sweeping her cheek. "Thank you."

He nodded.

"Oh, Cody, please believe me, I fully intend to end it. I'm being as completely honest as I know how."

"I know."

"You do?"

He nodded. He wrapped his arms around her and rested his chin on the crown of her head. "I don't know where that leaves us," he said. "Or even where we go from here."

"I don't, either," Christy whispered, but he felt her sigh of contentment as she relaxed against him.

"You're as jumpy as a grasshopper," Russ teased three nights later. "I swear you keep looking out that window as though you expect the Mounted Police to come riding over the hill any minute."

"Not the Mounted Police, just one incredibly handsome sheriff."

"Ah, so you're seeing Cody again tonight."

"I've seen him every night this week." Christy could feel herself blush as she said it, which was exactly the reaction her brother-in-law was looking for.

"Quit teasing my sister," Taylor said. She was sitting at the kitchen table. Eric was nestled in her arms, feeding greedily from her breast.

Every time Christy watched her sister with the baby, she was astonished at how easily Taylor had taken to being a mother. She acted as though she'd been around infants all her life, as if breast feeding were as natural as rain. Christy knew differently. The first attempts at the hospital to get Eric to cooperate had been frustrating ones. With the nurses' help and a whole lot of patience on Taylor's part, she'd finally managed to make it work for both her and Eric.

"Where's Cody taking you this afternoon?" Taylor asked, glancing up at her sister.

"He wouldn't say. It's supposed to be a surprise, but I have a sneaking suspicion we're headed into the wild blue yonder." At her sister's questioning glance, she explained. "I think he's planning to take me for a plane ride. He told me earlier he has his private license and twice now he's mentioned flying."

"I thought you were afraid of planes," Taylor commented. When it was first decided that Christy would come to Montana instead of their mother, the fact she should fly into Miles City was mentioned more than once. Christy had rejected the idea immediately. She had flown in the past, but wasn't keen on the idea. Driving to Montana appealed to her far more. Neither Taylor nor their mother had pressed the issue.

"I'm not excited about flying," Christy admitted.

"But you don't mind going up in a plane with Cody?"

"Not in the least." She trusted him beyond question. Enough to place her life in his hands and never doubt or fear.

"If I were you, I'd make sure his little surprise didn't involve horses," Russ warned, and his dark eyes connected with his wife's as though they were sharing some well-kept secret.

"Cody doesn't ride that often himself."

Russ poured himself a cup of coffee and joined Taylor at the kitchen table, twisting around a chair and straddling it. He propped his arms over the back and smiled at his son while speaking to Christy. "You certainly seem to know a great deal about the good sheriff's habits."

"I . . ." Christy could feel warmth invade her cheeks. She hated the easy way she blushed whenever the subject of Cody was introduced.

Russ was right about one thing. Cody and Christy had spent every available moment together. With the two weeks of her vacation vanishing like melting snow, each day was more precious than the one before. It was as if they were forced into cramming several months of a relationship into two short weeks.

Cody wasn't pleased with the fact that she remained technically engaged to James, but he'd graciously accepted the situation. It wasn't easy for him, but he never questioned her about the other man, or brought James into their conversation.

For his part, Cody had never said anything to Christy about Becca and the way he'd been duped by the other woman. She hadn't been looking for his confidence, but knowing what she did made her more sensitive to his needs and love him all the more.

Christy did love Cody. This wasn't infatuation or hormones or anything else. For some reason, unknown to them both, they were meant to be together. She knew it. He knew it. Yet Christy never spoke of her feelings, and neither did Cody.

She understood his hesitancy. He couldn't talk freely about what was between them, at least not while James remained a part of her life. Not when the attorney was waiting to place an engagement ring on her finger.

Once she was back in Seattle and had broken the engagement to James, then and only then would she tell Cody she loved him. He in turn would be free to tell her what she already knew.

Christy would have liked to hear it sooner, but if Cody could display a little patience, then she couldn't do anything less.

"I don't know what time we'll be back," Christy said, looking at her watch.

"Don't worry. I'm not going to wait up for you," Russ said, taking a sip of his coffee in what seemed like a blatant effort to conceal a smile.

"Is there anything I can do for you before I leave?" Christy asked, looking at Taylor.

Her sister grinned. "Just have a good time."

"I will." She was already having the time of her life.

"I was in town earlier today," Russ said, growing serious. He paused and glanced between the two women to be certain he had their full attention.

"You go into town twice a week or more," Taylor reminded him. She shared a suspicious look with Christy as if to question her husband's game.

"Noah Williams, who works at the insurance agency, stopped me." Once more he hesitated as if this bit of news was of a significant nature.

"Old man Williams stops anybody who will listen to him," Taylor interjected. "That man is the biggest gossip in three counties, and you know it."

Russ rubbed the side of his jaw in long, leisurely strokes. "Yeah, I suppose I do at that."

"Would you kindly say what's on your mind and be done with it?" Taylor grumbled.

Russ chuckled, clearly enjoying his game. "All right. Noah claimed he'd heard that the sheriff's about to take himself a wife. A right pretty one, too. He said word has it she's a relative of mine."

"Oh?" Christy asked, willingly playing into his hands. "And did this relative of yours have a name?"

Vaguely Christy recalled Cody introducing her to the town's sole insurance agent. She seemed to recall him telling her that Noah Williams was well acquainted with most folks' business whether they were his clients or not.

"Said he didn't recall the name, but he thought it was something like Cathy or Christine or Christabel."

"Funny. Very funny," Christy muttered, looking out the window, hoping to see the thin dust tail that followed Cody's truck down the bumpy driveway.

"I'm telling you right now," Russ said, chuckling as he spoke, "the secret's out. The sheriff's gonna take himself a wife."

Christy was lying on her back on the thick lawn, chewing on a long blade of grass. Cody lay beside her, staring at the darkening sky. A series of thick clouds were rolling in, obliterating the sun, but they'd both chosen to ignore the threat of rain.

"It looks like there's a storm brewing," Cody warned.

"Let it. I don't mind, do you?"

"That depends." He rolled onto his stomach and braced himself on his elbows as he gazed lovingly down at her. He didn't seem any more anxious to leave the site of their picnic than Christy.

The afternoon had been ideal in every way. Cody had arrived at the house early in the day, and Christy had met him with a basket packed full of goodies. Russ complained that she was taking enough food to feed a small army... of ants.

"Depends on what?" she pressed, smiling up at him.

"On who I'm with." As if he couldn't stop himself, he leaned over her and pressed his mouth to hers. He quickly rerouted his efforts, his lips moving along the side of her face and into her hair. He paused and went still as he breathed in the scent of the cologne she'd dabbed on the soft spot behind her ears.

Other than the few chaste kisses they'd shared infrequently over the past several days, Cody hadn't touched her. It wasn't that he didn't desire her, didn't need her. She had seen and felt the evidence of both. Yet he held himself in check as though he required the extra breathing room.

Christy understood and in many ways approved.

The physical attraction between them was more powerful than either had ever experienced. It wasn't something to be trifled with.

He kissed her again lightly, softly, gently.

Christy moved her hands up his chest and looped her arms around his neck. When he kissed her again, his breath was hot and quick.

"We should stop now," he warned, but he made no effort to move away from her.

"Yes, I know," she concurred.

He brushed his thumb back and forth over her moist lips as if gathering the needed resolve to pull away from her. She gazed up into his dark, troubled eyes and viewed his hesitation. His hands were trembling as he started to roll away from her.

"No." Her cry was instinctive. Urgent.

"Christy..."

"Shh." She sank her fingers into his hair at the sides of his rugged, lean face, raised her head from the soft patch of lawn and moved her mouth against his.

His hands tangled with her short curls as he moved the upper half of his body over hers, anchoring her to the ground. Low animal sounds emanated from deep within his throat. His tongue slid along hers, mating, deep, deeper, all the while aligning his mouth with hers, twisting and turning. He caught her lower lip between his teeth and sucked lightly before claiming her mouth again in a searing, hot exchange. When he broke away, they were both panting.

"Sweet heaven, tell me to stop," he pleaded. "Tell me...now."

Christy couldn't, not when she wanted him so desperately. Not when the hunger to love him all but consumed her. Fitfully she moved beneath him, parting her thighs. Cody groaned again as he nestled himself over her, his long legs bracketing hers.

"Christy," he pleaded anew, "we're headed for trouble if we don't stop... *now*."

"I thought sheriffs were trained to anticipate any and all types of trouble." Her tongue outlined his mouth even as she spoke, imitating the technique he'd used earlier. She caught his lower lip between her teeth, bit down lightly, then sucked hard, all the while mating her tongue with his.

"Dear, sweet Lord..." Cody groaned. His mouth moved over hers, licking, tasting, kissing until she thought she would go insane. His hands were busy with the buttons of her blouse, his movements jerky and slow, as though he expected her to stop him. After what seemed an eternity, he peeled aside the material of her western style shirt and freed the snap of her bra. Her breasts fell into his waiting hands, filling his palms.

Christy moaned.

Cody sighed.

His mouth fused with hers as his thumb caressed her nipples until they puckered and throbbed with a desire she couldn't name. His mouth left hers with reluctance, trailing slow, sensual kisses down the side of her neck and over her collarbone.

The heat of his kiss-dampened mouth closed firmly over her nipple. Christy bit into her lower lip and rolled her head to one side. Her chest heaved with this new realm of unexpected pleasure, and she plowed her fingers into his hair.

His tongue became an instrument of exquisite desire, an instrument of torture as his lips closed more firmly around her. He sucked hard until she whim-

pered and buckled beneath him, then he quickly
changed tactics, and the sucking action eased as he
lapped and washed the excited peak with gentle and not-
so-gentle tugs of his mouth.

Christy felt his desire, rock-hard, pressing against her
thigh. Her reaction was instinctive as she raised her hips
and started to move under him in slow, circular motions.

"Oh, baby, no..." he groaned, and shut his eyes.
Christy heard him gnash his teeth in an effort to con-
quer the desire, the need that had painfully gathered in
his loins.

"Please...don't stop," Christy begged. Her fingers
clawed his back.

"No..." he countered, but he made no effort to put
a stop to the rotation of her hips. Instead, he seemed to
be moving with her, pressing the rigid proof of his
manhood more boldly against her.

The vast differences in their bodies couldn't be denied. He was so hard. She was so soft.

His hungry lips found hers, and his tongue dipped
again and again into the dampness of her mouth, echo-
ing the movements of his thrusting hips.

Christy's breasts had never felt more full or more ripe
as when his hands closed over them. His thumbs re-
volved around the centers until her nipples went taut
and throbbed unmercifully.

It seemed as if there wasn't anything powerful enough
in this world or the next to pull them apart. Christy felt
as if she'd been created for this man, for this moment.
The loving between them was as inevitable as the setting sun. As natural as the ocean waves caressing the
shore.

She heard the snap give way to her jeans, felt his hand flatten against the smoothness of her stomach. His touch, his kiss, produced a powerful vibration in the very depths of her being.

The vibration grew more insistent until she realized something was amiss. It wasn't her blood that was pounding in her veins, but rain that was pounding the earth. The clouds burst over them, drenching Christy within seconds.

Cody stilled, his body tightening as he struggled with self-control. He slipped his hands from her breast to her face, framing it softly as he slowly raised his head. His passion-clouded gaze sought hers.

"Oh, Cody, it's raining something terrible."

He responded by kissing her. "You taste too damn sweet to move."

"You're getting drenched."

"So are you." He grinned. "And I don't mind if you don't."

"I don't."

"Good." Once more his mouth connected with hers. He pressed his tongue deep inside, kissing her hungrily.

Christy sagged against him. "We...almost made love."

"I promised myself we wouldn't," he whispered.

"So much for promises." She straightened and smiled up at him.

"This one I mean to keep." His hands closed around her upper arms. "Understand?"

Christy nodded.

"I mean it, Christy."

"Yes, sir." She teased him with a salute.

Deftly he reversed their positions, smoothly rolling over and taking her with him so she was poised above him. She straddled his hips and arched her head back as the rain pummeled her face. Brushing the hair away from her face, she smiled at the dark, angry sky.

"I suppose I should be grateful," Cody murmured.

"For the rain? Why?"

His fingers were agilely working the snap to her bra and the buttons of her shirt. "You know why."

"Yes," she whispered, "but in some ways I wish..." She let the rest fade, because they were aware of what would have happened if Mother Nature hadn't chosen to intervene when she did.

Chapter Seven

"You're sure you want to do this?" Taylor asked, turning expectantly toward Christy as though she expected her sister to call off the whole thing.

"You're going," Christy said, ushering her older sister toward the kitchen where Russ was waiting impatiently. It was the first time Taylor had left Eric, and she seemed to be having second thoughts.

"This night is for you and Russ."

"I know but—"

"I have the phone number to the restaurant, the home nurse, the doctor and the hospital. If anything the least bit out of the ordinary occurs, I'll phone someone, so quit worrying."

"Eric's never had a bottle," Taylor protested.

"It's still Mama's milk. He's a smart baby. He'll adjust." After spending a hilarious afternoon, learning how to operate the breast pump, each ounce was more precious than gold.

"Christy, I'm not so sure this is such a good idea, after all."

"Don't be ridiculous. Eric will probably sleep the entire time you're away."

"Are you going to let me take you to dinner or not?" Russ's voice boomed like a cannon from the kitchen. "I'd like to remind you the reservation is for six." After a hard day on the ranch, Russ got too hungry to wait much beyond that time for the evening meal.

Cody was the one who'd come up with the idea of the two of them baby-sitting Eric while Russ and Taylor took some time for themselves. It was Christy's last night in Cougar Point. First thing in the morning she would start the long drive across three states. Although she'd been gone less than two weeks, it felt as if an entire lifetime had passed.

"Cody's here," Russ called out. "Just how long is it going to take you women to put on a little war paint, anyway?" His voice lowered, and Christy could hear him conversing with the sheriff. Her brother-in-law was saying something along the lines that Taylor and Christy were the two most beautiful women in the county as it was. He contended that they didn't even need makeup, and he was having one hell of a time understanding why they bothered with it.

"Hold your horses," Taylor cried, sticking her head out the bathroom door and calling down the hallway into the kitchen. "I'll only be a minute."

"Those are famous last words if I ever heard them," Russ grumbled.

As it turned out, her brother-in-law was right. Taylor took an extra five minutes fussing with her hair and adding a dash of perfume to the pulse points at her wrists. When she'd finished, she checked Eric, gave Christy and Cody a long list of instructions that would have covered a week or more, then reluctantly left the house with her husband.

Cody wrapped his arm around Christy as they stood on the back porch, watching Russ hold open the car door for his wife. Christy smiled softly when Russ stole a lengthy kiss.

"Well," Cody said after Russ had pulled out of the yard, "they're off."

"I don't think they'll win any races."

"No," he chuckled, "I doubt that they will." He turned her into his arms and kissed her softly.

"Oh, honestly," Mandy said, scooting past them and down the porch steps. "You two are as bad as Russ and Taylor. If it was me doing these PDAs, you can bet I'd be in big trouble. It seems to me that those over twenty-one can get away with a whole lot more than they should."

"PDAs?" Christy asked, confused.

"Public Displays of Affection," Cody whispered close to her ear. As if the temptation were too strong to resist, he caught her lobe between his teeth and bit down lightly.

"Cody," Christy cried, slapping his backside, "behave yourself."

"Hey, where are you going?" Cody demanded when Mandy started toward the barn. "I thought you were going to stick around and chaperone the two of us."

"I'm headed for the movies."

"In the barn?"

"Don't be cute with me, Cody Franklin. Just because you've been elected sheriff doesn't mean you can control my life. So don't try to get funny with me."

Cody moved behind Christy and wrapped his arms around her waist. "You're not the one I want to get cute with."

"Obviously. I thought you two would appreciate a little privacy. Billy Joe's driving me over to Melissa's. She got her driver's license last week."

"I heard rumors along those lines," Cody said with a cocky grin.

"Just don't go sending Bud or any of the other deputies out to tail us." Mandy wagged an accusing finger in Cody's direction. "I know you'd do it, too, if you thought you could get away with it. Melissa's just a little nervous yet, and the last thing she needs is a sheriff's car following her into town."

"You think I'd radio for someone to follow her?" Cody sounded aghast that Mandy would even hint at something so dastardly.

"You'd do it if you thought you could." But Russ's teenage sister was smiling as she spoke.

Billy Joe stepped out from the barn, freshly shaved. His hair was wet and combed down against the sides of his head. "You ready?"

"Anytime," Mandy said, walking toward the hired hand's battered red pickup.

From what Taylor had explained, Russ's foreman was sweet on Melissa's widowed mother and had been courting her for the past several months. Apparently Mandy and Melissa were working together to stage an evening alone for the two adults.

Eric started to fuss, and after bidding Mandy farewell, Christy hurried inside the house and into the master bedroom. Eric was lying in the bassinet, dutifully waiting for someone to answer his beck and call.

"What's the matter, big boy?" she asked softly, reaching for him. His damp bottom answered that question. "So you wet your diaper, did you?" she chided playfully, giving him her finger, which he promptly gripped.

"I'll change him," Cody offered from behind her.

Christy arched finely shaped brows in feigned shock. "This I've got to see."

"I'll have you know I've worked my way around more than one diaper in my lifetime."

"That may be true, but it seems to me you took great delight in teasing Russ when he offered to change Eric."

"I've had more practice than Russ, that's all." Cody reached for a fresh diaper from the pile of folded ones stacked on the dresser top. "Both of my sisters have children, and being the generous uncle I am, I've lent a hand now and again. It's not nearly as difficult as Russ made it out to be."

"All right, since you're so confident, go ahead and I'll see to our dinner." Carefully she handed Cody the baby, then headed for the kitchen.

Taylor had set out a pepperoni pizza to thaw on the kitchen counter. The only place in Cougar Point that served pizza was the bowling alley, and Taylor could go without a lot of the modern luxuries, but she needed her pizza. Every time she was in Miles City, she bought three or four pepperoni pizzas from a nationwide chain, brought them home and promptly froze them.

"I hope you're in the mood for pizza," Christy called, setting the gauge on the oven to the right temperature.

"You mean to say Taylor's willing to share one of hers? Without us even having to ask?"

"I didn't even have to bribe her."

"I may volunteer to baby-sit more often," Cody said as he walked into the kitchen, holding Eric against his shoulder. His large hand was pressed against the infant's tiny back, whose head rested against Cody's muscular shoulder.

Christy paused when she saw them, and her heart beat so hard, it pained her chest. Cody looked so natural with a baby in his arms. As natural as any father. Turning away in an effort to disguise the emotion that clawed at her, she gripped the counter with both hands and waited for the aching tenderness to pass.

She was engaged to an attorney in Seattle, a good friend she'd known for several years, and not once had she pictured him as a father. The fact they'd most likely have children someday hadn't so much as crossed her mind.

Yet here she was alone with Cody and her nephew, and the sight of this lean-hipped, rugged man holding this precious child was enough to bring tears to her eyes.

"Christy, could you hand me..." He paused when she didn't immediate respond. "Christy?"

She swallowed the lump in her throat, smeared the moisture across her cheek and turned around, smiling as brightly as she could. She doubted she was going to be able to fool Cody, but she felt the need to try.

"What's wrong?" His question was tender and filled with concern.

"Nothing..."

"If that's the case, then why are you crying?"

She didn't know any way she could explain it, not without sounding as though she required long-term therapy. She was crazy in love with one man, and engaged to another. In a few short hours she was going to be leaving Cody behind. There were no guarantees, no pledges, no promises between them.

Nothing.

There couldn't be anything while she remained engaged to James.

James. Two weeks away from him and she had trouble remembering what he looked like. What did fill her mind was the fact he drank his tea with milk and hadn't donned a pair of jeans since he was thirteen years old. He was endearing, hardworking and brilliant.

And he loved her. At least he thought he did, the same way she'd once assumed she loved him.

The phone rang, and the sound of it startled Eric, who let out a loud wail. Cody whispered reassurances while gently patting the baby's back.

"I'll get that," Christy said, grateful for the intrusion, grateful to delay answering Cody's questions. "No doubt it's Taylor wanting to check up on us." She hurried into the hallway, wanting to catch the phone before it rang again and frightened Eric a second time.

"Hello," she greeted cheerfully. "This is Palmer's Pizza Parlor. May I take your order?" Taylor was sure to get a kick out of that.

A short, abrupt silence followed her salutation.

"It appears I've dialed the wrong number," a male voice stated stiffly.

"James? Oh, dear...I thought it was Taylor phoning. This is Christy."

Cody heard the bubbling laughter drain out of Christy two seconds after she answered the phone. It didn't take long for him to realize that the man on the other end of the line was Christy's fiancé.

Before he even realized it, Cody was swamped with confusion and an equally large dose of good old-fashioned jealousy. He was so damn resentful of Christy's engagement to the other man that a second pain-filled moment passed before he was able to clear his head. He'd never been the jealous type, and now he was all but blinded by the powerful emotion.

It shouldn't have been a surprise to him that James—he had trouble thinking about the other man without it tightening his jaw—would contact Christy. If Cody was the one engaged to her and she was a thousand miles away, he'd phone her, too. Frequently.

That realization, however, was little comfort. Before too many more hours passed, Christy would be leaving Cougar Point. Within two days' time she'd be back with James. Her weeks with him in Montana would be a little more than a fading memory.

Cody wasn't willing to kid himself any longer. There wasn't any use trying to hide from it, or deny it or attempt to ignore it. He was in love with Christy Manning. A thousand times he pledged he'd never allow this foolish emotion to take hold of his life again. So much for all the promises he'd made himself. So much for protecting his heart.

Damn it all, he was in love!

But Cody was realistic enough to put their relationship in the proper perspective. Or at least try to. Christy was engaged to a hotshot Seattle attorney. He, on the other hand, was a backwoods sheriff. Christy may be infatuated with him now, but once she returned to the big city that could all easily change. Believing these few days together would mean something more to her could be dangerous thinking on his part.

She was going to break the engagement. Or so she claimed. But now something was suddenly troubling her. Cody had sensed it when she was fussing with the pizza. When he'd first arrived, she'd been her warm, happy self. She'd teased and joked with him as though she hadn't a care in the world. She'd been too happy. Too carefree.

Cody frowned. Since the afternoon of their picnic when they'd gotten caught in the downpour, Cody had noted several subtle changes in her. She seemed more spontaneous, more open with him.

He was willing to admit there had been numerous intricate transformations in their relationship over the past ten days. They'd spent a good deal of time together, getting to know each other, growing to love each other.

And for most of that time Cody had had one hell of a time keeping his eyes and his hands off her.

Christy Manning was the most beautiful, graceful creature who'd ever come into his life. He found himself studying her at every opportunity, and each time he did he liked what he saw. She completely and totally captivated him. When they were alone together, he'd learned how dangerous it was to kiss her, or more appropriately to stop kissing her. She would press her soft body to his, and it was a test by fire of his limited control.

In the distance Cody heard the anxiety in her voice as Christy's phone conversation continued with the other man. Not willing to listen in, Cody opened the screen door and walked outside. He sat on the top step and let his gaze wander across the acres of prime pasture land that made up the Lazy P.

"See all those pesky cattle, Eric?" he whispered to the baby held securely against his shoulder. "It'll all belong to you someday. Take some advice, though, boy..." He was about to tell Russ's son not to get involved with women because all they did was cause a man grief.

Cody stopped himself just in time. Christy hadn't caused him trouble. If anything, she was like a ray of warm sunshine after a long, cold winter. He hadn't realized how lonely he'd become over the past several years. Nor had he sensed how isolated his life had become until she walked into it, bold as could be.

Okay, he mused, sighing deeply. He was in love. It wasn't supposed to happen, but it had. Damn if he knew what to do next. For a man in his thirties he'd had precious little experience with the emotion. The one other time he'd committed his heart to a woman, it had cost him dearly. He hadn't been willing to place himself at risk a second time until he met Christy.

Fifteen minutes, or more fitting, an eternity, passed before Christy finally joined him. He heard her moving behind him in the kitchen and felt the swish of the screen door as it opened.

"That was James," she said softly as she sat down on the concrete step beside him.

"I heard." He sounded flippant, uncaring.

"He...he's called two other times."

"That's none of my business," he informed her curtly.

"I know, but I want to be as honest with you as I can be. Are you angry?"

"No."

"You sound angry."

"I'm not." And pigs fly, he told himself.

For a long moment Christy didn't say anything. She sat there looking like an angel, smelling like something directly out of a garden of roses. How was a man supposed to resist her when she looked over at him with those incredible blue eyes of hers? Hell, if Cody knew...

"I...almost told him about you. It was on the tip of my tongue to try to explain about meeting you, but James seemed so preoccupied. He was visiting my parents, and I spoke to them, too, and that made it all the more difficult."

"Why's that?" He made a determined effort to take the starch out of his voice.

She hesitated before answering. "My mom and dad like James a lot."

"I'm sure he's perfect son-in-law material."

Christy ignored that comment, which was probably best. He knew he wasn't dealing with this situation well. In fact, he was making a real jackass of himself.

"Now...now that I've had these two weeks with you, I think I accepted his proposal more to please my parents than because I was in love with James."

"I see." A series of immediate questions popped into his mind. Christy was a kind person, affectionate and empathetic, gentle and good.

"They like Russ, too," she hurried to add.

Cody didn't know what that proved, and frankly he wasn't in the frame of mind to ask.

"Or at least they do now. At first—" she stopped abruptly, as if she'd already said too much.

Knowing what he did about her, Cody didn't doubt that the week to come, when she confronted James and her family, would be one of the most difficult of her life. That is, if she went through with it, if she did decide to break off the engagement, after all.

"I ... can't bear for us to spend our last night together arguing," she whispered softly.

Cody forced himself to relax. He couldn't bear it, either. He lifted his free arm and lopped it around her shoulders, drawing her closer to him and Eric. She turned and shyly smiled up at him. With unhurried ease he lowered his head until their mouths met. Her lips parted in enthusiastic welcome, and his tongue sought hers. The kiss was long, slow and thorough, so thorough that when he lifted his head, Cody felt light-headed and dizzy with longing.

"Oh, Cody," she moaned, her fingers closing around his shirt collar, her eyes closed, "I hate to leave you."

He hated it, too, feared it more than he'd feared anything. He dreaded the moment she would drive away from him.

Fear and dread. Fighting those emotions was one hell of a way to spend their last hours together.

"Are you sure you haven't forgotten something?" Taylor asked for the tenth time in as many minutes. They stood beside Christy's car, Taylor in her housecoat, Christy in her traveling clothes—a comfortable pair of faded jeans and a ten-button henley shirt.

"I'm sure I've got everything." She'd checked the house twice, and even if she had inadvertently missed something, she'd be back. Soon, she hoped. As soon as she could clear up the situation with James. As soon as she was free.

Taylor hugged her close, and Russ stepped forward, holding Eric. He placed his free arm around Christy and squeezed tight.

"Drive carefully," Taylor said, "and phone the minute you arrive in Seattle. You know I'll worry until I hear from you." Tears brimmed from her sister's eyes as she reached for and hugged Christy one last time. "Damn, I hate to see you go."

"I'll phone first thing," Christy promised. As for the part about hating to leave, that went without saying. This was far more difficult than she imagined it would be.

"Where's Cody?" Russ asked, frowning.

"He's got the day shift," Christy explained. They'd said their farewells earlier. Although she'd spent until the wee hours of the morning saying goodbye to the sheriff, she half expected Cody to come barreling down the driveway before she headed out. She wasn't overly disappointed that he hadn't come, but a little despite her best efforts not to be.

"Be a good little baby," she whispered to Eric, and kissed his powder-scented brow. "Remember your Aunt Christy." With no more reason to delay, she opened her car door and climbed inside.

As she was driving away, Christy looked in the rearview mirror and caught sight of Taylor slipping her arm around her husband's waist. She pressed her head to his broad chest and leaned against him as though to absorb his strength.

The scene was a touching one, and Christy found herself blinking back tears.

She was still fighting back the emotion, and sniffled every now and again as she headed toward the highway that would connect her with the freeway. It would be a straight shot to Seattle after that.

Christy planned to make the best time she could. The sooner she was home, the sooner she could set her life in order.

Reaching across the seat, she located the thermos of coffee Taylor had insisted she take with her. Holding it between her legs, she struggled to unscrew the cap. It was difficult to do with one hand. She'd just about given up and was battling with the frustration and an acute sense of loss when a flashing blue and red light was reflected in her rearview mirror.

Cody.

Christy eased to the side of the road, turned off the engine and threw open the door. It was impossible to hold her emotions at bay a moment longer.

Her gaze was blurred with tears, but it didn't matter. Cody had come to her, and from the speed with which his patrol car had overtaken hers, he'd been in an almighty rush to find her.

By the time she'd climbed out of the car, Cody was out of his. Not waiting for an invitation, she rushed toward him, sobbing, so grateful he'd come.

Cody caught her, encircling her waist with his arms and lifting her from the ground in one fell swoop. His lips found hers, their mouths connecting with such force that it threw her head back. Christy didn't mind; she was as needy as Cody. As hungry. As lost. As afraid.

He continued to kiss her, saying with his body what he couldn't with words. That he loved her, needed her and was desperately afraid of losing her.

Christy understood and responded to each doubt.

"There's a side road about two miles back. Do you know where I mean?"

She nodded, remembered having driven past it minutes earlier.

"Meet me there?"

"Yes."

By the time she climbed back into her car, Christy was trembling from the inside out like a wind-tossed leaf. Her stomach felt tight, and her heart was pounding like a crazed jackhammer. Cody made a U-turn and led the way. Christy willingly followed.

He pulled onto the dirt road, stirring up several layers of fine dust, momentarily obliterating his vehicle. He drove a short way past a wide curve, then he pulled over to the side. Christy watched as he reached for his radio. She climbed out of her car and waited for him.

"I told dispatch I wouldn't be available for the next fifteen minutes," he explained, his dark eyes holding her captive. "I know it's not near enough time to say what I want, but it's all the time I dare take."

Christy nodded.

He gently brushed his fingertips over her damp cheek. "You've been crying."

"I . . . couldn't get the thermos open."

"That's why?" he questioned softly.

"No, it's not. I don't want to go. Oh, Cody, it's so much harder to leave you than I thought it would be." She tried unsuccessfully to swallow a sob.

"Don't cry," Cody pleaded. "I can't bear it." He held her against his chest and lowered his head. When he kissed her, the action was marked by desperation and urgency, his mouth slanting over hers. Her knees liquified. She clung to him, giving as much as she was taking, mating her tongue with his plundering one.

Cody lifted her as though she weighed nothing, and set her on the hood of her car so that her face was level with his own. Already her nipples were beaded and hard, throbbing with need. He buried his face in the curve of her neck and drew in several deep breaths.

"I need to taste you?" He made the statement a question as if he feared her response. As if he were asking too much of her, stretching the limit of how far he should go with her.

"Yes...please," she whispered, having trouble finding her voice.

His eyes followed the long row of dainty buttons that made up the front of her shirt, and paused at the beaded hardness of her nipples.

Without waiting for him Christy reached behind her and freed the snap of her bra. Her breasts sprang free, filling the front of her thin shirt, which she slowly removed. Cody couldn't seem to take his eyes away from her.

"You are so beautiful," he whispered, and his voice was tight with emotion. Slowly, as if having lost a battle with himself, he raised his hands to her breasts, covering them, molding them to fit inside his palms. Gently he bunched them, drawing their fullness together.

He kissed her neck, nuzzled it. Christy let her head fall back, allowing him freer access to do whatever he wished. She was his for this moment, this hour, this day.

His warm mouth skimmed the velvet length of her throat, planting moist kisses along her shoulder blade...then lower, much lower.

Christy released a ragged sigh of pleasure as his mouth closed firmly over her breast, taking in as much of it as humanly possible. She plowed her fingers through his hair as he divided his attention between one and the other, creating a friction that sparked fire and need.

Slowly, as if he were calling upon every ounce of self-control he possessed, Cody lifted his head. His eyes were as dark as she had ever seen them, wide and perceptive.

"Letting you go is the hardest thing I've ever done," he whispered. He smoothed the hair away from her face and kissed her, his tongue mating with hers until the kiss threatened to send them both out of control. Christy heard her own murmur of desire that was soon echoed by Cody.

A well-modulated voice came over the radio of the patrol car, reminding them both who and what Cody was. A defender of justice, a man who had pledged to protect and serve. As much as he would have liked to stay with her, to love her completely, the time had come for them both to return to their lives.

He helped her dress, his actions slow and deliberate as if to delay the inevitable.

"I'll follow you to the county line," he told her, lifting her off the car. He held open her car door for her, looking very much like the dignified sheriff he was. There was little evidence of the loving interlude that had passed between them.

A nod was all Christy could manage. She climbed into the driver's seat. Her hand closed around the key. Cody held on to her door, his eyes trained directly ahead and unreadable.

"I guess this is goodbye then," she said hoarsely. "At least for now."

He nodded. "For now. You'll drive carefully?"

"Of course."

Again he nodded, softly closed her door and then stepped back. He seemed about to say something more, but apparently changed his mind.

Christy waited for him to enter his patrol car before starting her engine. She offered him a smile and glanced in her rearview mirror to smile at him before she entered the main road.

True to his word, Cody followed her for several miles. In the distance she read the sign that stated she was leaving Custer County. An immediate knot formed in her throat, making it difficult to swallow.

A glance in her rearview mirror showed Cody's red and blue lights were flashing. She pulled over and stopped. Cody eased the patrol car in behind her.

He was out of his vehicle before she had a chance to free her seat belt. Rolling down her side window, she looked to him expectantly.

"One last thing before you go." His voice was deep and gravelly. "I love you, Christy. Come back to me."

Chapter Eight

"James," Christy said softly, her blue eyes tender and concerned, "you know I consider you one of my dearest friends. I've always heard good friends make the very best husbands...no," she mumbled, her hands closing more tightly around the steering wheel. "That doesn't sound the least bit right. Think, Christy, think!"

She'd just crossed the Idaho-Washington border and was within six hours of Seattle, and her home. Every mile, every minute, led her closer to the confrontation with James and her parents.

For the past two days Christy had carefully rehearsed what she planned to say, outlining her speech, inordinately conscious of each word that would pass her lips and how difficult her task would be.

James would be devastated, her parents shocked.

When it came right down to it, Christy was more worried about confronting her parents than she was James, especially her father, whom she adored. Eric Manning always seemed to know what was best for her, and for the most part, Christy had agreed. And he'd decided James would be the perfect husband for his youngest daughter.

The hours sped past, far too quickly to suit Christy. She found as she approached the outskirts of Seattle that she was traveling well below the speed limit, which produced several heated stares from her fellow travelers.

Once she arrived at her apartment building and had unloaded her car, Christy paced her living room with all the enthusiasm of a drill instructor. She'd assumed that once she was surrounded by everything that was familiar, some of the restless uneasiness would leave her.

It didn't. In fact, she was more agitated now than ever.

Gathering her courage, she decided to contact her family and deal with them first. She planned to ask if it was convenient for her to come over, hoping it would be. The she could quickly put an end to this madness.

Once she was alone with her parents, she could tell them she intended to break the engagement to James. Her argument was prepared, her decision unshakable.

Her first choice would have been to do it over the phone, but that would be a cowardly way out. Her only option was to confront them both together. Once that was finished she would deal with James.

She reached for her phone, astonished at the way her stomach tightened. She wasn't sure what to expect from either party and tried not to dwell on how they would react to her news. Planting her hand over her abdomen, she closed her eyes and prayed someone would answer before she lost her courage and hung up the phone.

"Hello."

"Jason?" He was her second oldest brother and the most handsome of the lot, or so he liked to claim. At thirty-two he was a "catch," only he enjoyed playing the field far too much to settle down with any one woman.

"Christy? When did you get back?"

"Just a few minutes ago." How odd she sounded. Christy prayed Jason wouldn't notice. "Are Mom and Dad around?"

"They will be soon. You don't know yet, do you?"

"Know what?" Jason loved playing games, dangling bits and pieces of information in front of her like bait, making her hungry for more.

"Never mind."

"Jason, I've been on the road for two days, and to be frank, I'm not up to any of your trick questions." Under normal circumstances Christy would have been amused and played along, but not now.

"Hey, sweetie, there are no trick questions with this one. All I can say is you have one hell of a surprise waiting for you. Mom has slaved every day since you've been gone, so if I were you, I'd make my presence known soon."

"Thank you so much," Christy muttered sarcastically. "Talking to you is like looking through a telescope with the lens cap on."

"Always happy to oblige," Jason responded with a light chuckle. "Just drop by the house soon.... In fact, the sooner the better."

Christy intended on doing exactly that. "I'll be over in fifteen minutes. By the way, how's Mom?" Breaking her leg had set Elizabeth Manning back several weeks, and Christy knew how terribly disappointed her mother had been to miss spending this important time with her eldest daughter and her newborn grandson.

"Mom's doing great. Especially now..." He didn't finish the enigmatic statement, and Christy refused to fall into his hands by asking him what he meant. "If you don't mind, I'll stick around myself for a while. I'd like to get a look at your face once you find out what's been going on around here. Mom's in seventh heaven. At the rate things are going, you're likely to end up with your pretty face issued across a first-class stamp."

"Cute, Jason, real cute." Christy hadn't a clue what he was talking about, but that was typical of her older brother. Over the last several years, his tongue had taken on a biting edge. Christy didn't know what his problem was, but she wished he'd straighten out whatever was wrong.

In an effort to delay the unavoidable, Christy played back the messages on her answering machine while she leafed through two weeks of mail. Anyone who mattered wouldn't have phoned because they'd know she was out of town, but she couldn't help being curious.

There were several beeps, indicating that whoever had called had hung up before leaving a message. Probably salesmen.

Deciding it was a waste of time, Christy started for her front door when Taylor's voice, hesitant and unsure, came over the tiny speaker. "Christy, call me as soon as you get home. Something's up that we need to discuss."

There was an uncharacteristic note in her sister's voice, a pause, an uncertainty that made her sound as though something was terribly amiss.

Puzzled, Christy returned to the phone and placed a long-distance call to Cougar Point. Mandy answered the phone, sounding as chipper and cheerful as ever.

"Taylor's not here," Russ's sister explained. "She drove into Miles City for Eric's first appointment with the pediatrician. Do you want me to have her call you once she gets back? I don't think it'll be too much longer. I know she was anxious to talk to you."

"No. I'm headed to my parents' house now. I'll phone again later." Hopefully by that time everything would be settled. She could contact Taylor and Russ and then talk to Cody. The mere thought of the sheriff caused her to go weak inside. Seemingly by accident they'd found each other and unexpectedly discovered what it meant to fall in love. Neither of them had been looking for this, neither of them fully understood why it had happened, but it was right. Right for Cody. Right for Christy.

After two long days on the road, she was physically exhausted and mentally depleted. Some would suggest that she delay this confrontation until she was well rested and relaxed. Christy disagreed. The engagement to James hung over her head like a threatening thundercloud. She wouldn't find peace until everything was cleared out of the road that would lead her back to her sheriff.

Her parents' luxury vehicle was parked in the driveway when Christy arrived. Jason's car was in the street, and Christy eased her own behind his. Even before she'd turned off the engine, her father had opened the front door and was walking toward her, his arms outstretched.

Eric Manning embraced his daughter, hugging her close. From the time she was little Christy had always felt a special closeness to her parents. Most of her friends had rebelled in one way or another against their families and authority, but never Christy. She'd never felt the need.

"When did you get back?" her father asked.

"Less than a half hour ago." She slipped her arm around his thickening waist as they walked toward the sprawling brick house. The lawn was green and freshly mowed. Many a happy hour had been spent racing across this same patch of green. Echoes of her childhood laughter seemed to mock her now.

Elizabeth Manning stood in the entryway, her left leg encased from her foot to just below her knee in a hot pink cast. Her face broke into a broad smile as Christy approached the front door.

"Sweetheart, it's so good to have you home."

"It's good to be home, and before you ask, yes, I brought tons of pictures of Eric."

"Oh, good, I can't tell you how excited we are that Russ and Taylor named him after your father."

Christy stepped into the house. It was a large home built into a hill overlooking the freeway that sliced a wide path through the heart of Seattle. The basement opened onto an enormous, landscaped yard with a profusion of flower beds and a vast space for a garden, whose bounty spilled over to several friends and neighbors every summer.

"How's the leg?"

"Better," Elizabeth claimed, discounting her daughter's concern with a quick shake of her head. She was walking with a cane now, leaning heavily upon it. Christy knew her mother well enough to realize Elizabeth Manning would never want to burden her children with the fact she was in a good deal of pain. But her mother did look chipper, Christy mused. The sparkle was back in her eyes, and a flush of excitement glowed from her cheeks. In fact, Christy couldn't remember how long it had been since she'd seen her mother look quite so pleased. No doubt the birth of their third grandson was responsible for this happiness.

"You're looking wonderful," Christy said, kissing her mother's rosy cheek.

"Actually, sweetie, we have you to thank for that," her father supplied, sharing an enigmatic smile with wife.

"I'm the one responsible?" Apparently her parents were playing the same game as Jason.

"Eric, let's not discuss this in the entryway."

Her father chuckled, and Christy noted that his eyes seemed brighter, too. He certainly was in one of his better moods. Christy would like to think it was all due to her arrival and the fact she'd brought pictures of their grandson. But somehow she doubted that was the case, especially after having spoken to Jason.

Her second oldest brother was sitting in the family room in front of the television when Christy walked in. He was wearing a Seattle Mariners baseball cap, which he donned a majority of the time.

"Welcome home, little sister," he greeted. He stood and dutifully hugged her. Then he stepped back and wiggled his eyebrows several times.

"All right, you guys," Christy said, claiming the easy chair next to her brother. "What's going on around here?"

The edges of her father's mouth started to quiver as though he was having a difficult time holding back his excitement. Once more he shared a look with his wife of thirty-five years.

"If you'll recall, your mother's spirits were low after she fell and broke her leg. Missing out on this special time with Taylor and Russ depressed her terribly."

"I didn't even realize how melancholy I'd become until Eric mentioned it," Elizabeth explained. "Sometimes I swear he knows me better than I know myself."

Christy felt herself nod.

"Your father's the one who came up with the idea for the engagement party."

"An engagement party," Christy echoed, coming halfway out of her chair, appalled and dismayed.

Her mother pressed her fingertips over her lips, almost giddy with delight. "We knew you'd be pleased."

"I...I..." Christy was at a complete loss for words. Somehow she managed a smile and slumped back into the thick cushions of the overstuffed chair.

"You can't imagine what fun we've had," Elizabeth continued, her voice animated. "I'm afraid your father got carried away. He insisted we order the best of everything. We've rented the Eagles Hall, got the invitations mailed, engraved ones. Oh sweetie, I can hardly wait for you to see them. We spent hour upon hour with the caterers. I can't even begin to tell you what a fabulous time I...we had planning every detail of this party. I can't help feeling proud of everything we accomplished in so short a time."

"It was just what the doctor ordered for your mother," Christy's father inserted smoothly, looking equally delighted. "Elizabeth's been like a kid again from the moment we decided to go through with this."

"I see." Christy went completely numb. An earthquake wouldn't have moved her. It seemed impossible that no one noticed.

"I suppose we're both a pair of old fools, but when Taylor married Russ in Reno, your father and I felt cheated out of a large family wedding. We've been looking forward to throwing one for years."

"When?" It was torture getting the one word past the growing tightness that all but blocked her throat.

"That's the crazy part," Jason said. "Mom and Dad put this entire thing together in two weeks."

Still Christy didn't understand, but there was very little of the conversation that made a whole lot of sense. Her look must have conveyed her confusion.

"The party's tomorrow night," Elizabeth explained, her face radiating her excitement.

"Tomorrow night?"

"I know it sounds crazy, and we took a hell of a chance booking it so close to the end of your vacation, but there were only a few dates available at the Eagles Hall, and it was either tomorrow night or three months from now."

"In fact, the only reason we were able to get the hall is because of a last-minute cancellation," Eric explained. "I had no idea we'd need to book this sort of thing so much in advance."

"James?" No one seemed to notice how she was having trouble speaking, which Christy supposed was a blessing in disguise.

"He knows, of course, but we'd decided to keep it a secret for you. A welcome home surprise, if you will."

Christy nodded, hating the way she continued to sit in her parents' home and say nothing when it felt as if the foundations to her world were crumbling at her feet. Her mother and father and Jason were all looking at her, waiting for some response, but for the life of her, Christy couldn't give them one.

Her gaze connected with her brother's.

He winked broadly. "Mom and Dad are sparing no expense. If the wedding is half as elaborate as the engagement party, then your big day's going to rival Charles and Diana's."

Eric Manning chuckled loudly. "It isn't every father who had a daughter as special as Christy."

Christy forced a smile when on the inside she longed to stand up and cry out for them to put an end to this craziness. She didn't love James. She loved Cody. She couldn't possibly go through with an engagement party to a man she didn't intend to marry.

She glanced from her mother to her father, both of whom seemed to be staring at her with bright, eager smiles, as though waiting for her to burst into a song of praise for their multiple efforts.

"I...I..." The words froze on her lips.

"Honey, look," Elizabeth murmured devotedly to her husband. "Christy's speechless. Oh, sweetie, you don't need to say anything. Your father and I understand. If anyone should be giving thanks, it's me. I was so miserable after my fall. Planning this party was the best thing in the world for me. I've loved every minute of it. Keeping it a surprise has been so much fun."

There had to be a plausible excuse she could use not to go through with this farce of an engagement party.

"I don't have a dress." The words escaped her lips almost as quickly as they formed in her mind.

"Not to worry," Elizabeth countered, her eyes glowing even brighter. "I thought of everything, even if I do say so myself. I went shopping the other day and picked out a dress for you myself. If you don't like it, or it doesn't fit, then we can exchange it first thing in the morning."

First thing in the morning. The words echoed in her ears like a Chinese gong. "I...I'm supposed to go back to work." That sounded reasonable to her. After two weeks away from the law firm, Christy was expected back. They needed her. They were short-staffed without her. She couldn't demand additional time off to exchange a party dress.

"No need to worry about that, either," Eric said brightly. "James has that corner covered. He talked it over with the office manager, and she's given you two extra days off with pay."

"Tomorrow, of course, will be filled with all the last-minute details for the party," Elizabeth explained, excitedly rubbing her palms together as if she were a teenager all over again.

"You didn't tell Taylor?" Her older sister would have said something to her; Christy was convinced of it.

"Well, not right away. I mailed her a long letter and an invitation so that it would arrive the day you were scheduled to leave Montana. I'm sure she has it by now. I couldn't take the chance of mailing it sooner for fear you'd find it, and I didn't want to say anything when we phoned for fear she'd inadvertently let the cat out of the bag. I did so want to keep this a surprise."

"I see," Christy murmured.

"Your father and I don't expect Taylor to fly home for the party, not so soon after having the baby. I'm sure she and Russ will come out for the wedding. Which is something else we need to discuss. Talk to James, sweetie—the sooner we have a date for the actual wedding, the better it will be. There's so much to do, and I so want this wedding to be carefully planned. I can't tell you everything I've learned the past two weeks. The first thing after the party tomorrow night, we're going to sit down and discuss the wedding."

Christy nodded, simply because she lacked the courage to explain there would never be a wedding, at least not one in which James was the bridegroom.

"You are surprised, aren't you?" Jason demanded, looking exceptionally cocky, as if he were the one responsible for pulling this whole affair together.

Surprise was too mild a word for what Christy was experiencing. Even shock and dismay were too mild.

Horror and panic more aptly described her feelings.

James! She needed to talk to James. He'd help her. He'd understand, and then together they'd clear up this mess. Together they could confront her parents and make them understand.

She stood before she realized what she was doing. It seemed everyone in the room was staring holes straight through her. Glancing around, she offered them each a weak smile.

Always dutiful. Always obedient. Never causing a concern or a problem. For the first time in her life Christy was about to destroy her good-girl image.

But first she had to talk to James.

Two messages were waiting for Christy on her answering machine when she returned later that same afternoon. The first was from Cody and the second from Taylor.

Christy didn't answer either.

Instead she sat in her living room, staring into space, loaded down with an incredible weight, pressured beyond anything she'd ever experienced and entangled in circumstances beyond her control.

How long she stayed in her living room Christy didn't know. Here she was safe. Here she was protected. Here she could hide.

That small sense of security, however, quickly disintegrated. Knowing there was nothing else she could do to stop the progression of events, she stood and walked into the kitchen. She paused in front of the phone, then abruptly reached for it before she had a change of heart.

Cody wasn't home, and she left an all too brief message on his phone. Her next call was to Taylor.

"Christy, dear heaven, what's going on?" Taylor demanded the instant she recognized it was her younger sister. "I got this crazy letter from Mom about her planning a surprise engagement party for you. What's happening?"

"You mean about the party?" Christy asked, shocked that her voice lacked any level of emotion. She had none left.

"Of course I mean the party," Taylor cried. "Do you mean to say you're going through with it?"

"I don't have any choice."

"Christy, you can't be serious! What about Cody? I thought you were in love with him. I may be stepping out of line here, but I could have sworn you..." She paused, inhaling deeply. "I better stop before I say something I shouldn't. Just answer me one question. Do you or do you not love Cody Franklin?"

Christy wiped the moisture from her face and nodded wildly. "You know I do."

"Then it seems to me you're allowing Mom and Dad to dictate your life."

"You don't understand," Christy whimpered, having difficulty keeping her voice from quavering.

"What's there to understand?"

"Mom broke her leg..." She paused, unable to go on, wondering if she should even try to untangle this terrible mess. Even if she did it was doubtful Taylor would understand.

"Mom's accident isn't any surprise to me," Taylor returned impatiently.

"Mom was terribly depressed afterward. I saw it, we all did, but apparently it didn't go away like everyone expected it would. Then Dad came up with the brilliant idea of putting together this engagement party."

"Oh, dear."

"Mom put everything she had into it, and now—"

"Christy, I know it's difficult, but you've got to remember Mom and Dad planned this party without consulting you."

That was true enough, but it didn't change the facts. "I can't humiliate them. I thought if I talked to James, told him about Cody, everything would work out, but then I discovered I couldn't do that, either. I wanted us to face Mom and Dad and make some kind of decision together about the party, but that's impossible now. Everything's so crazy... I can't believe this is happening."

"Do you mean to say James doesn't know about Cody?"

Christy's eyes slammed closed.

"Christy?"

"I...couldn't tell him." Christy stiffened, waiting for the backlash of anger that was sure to follow.

A short but profound silence followed her words. "You *couldn't* tell James about Cody?"

The trouble she had forming the words was painfully obvious. "You heard me right."

Another short silence followed, this one wounded and heavy. "I see."

"How could you possibly *see*?" Christy demanded, keeping her voice level, when she wanted to scream at the accusation she heard in her own sister's voice. "I went to him, fully intending on telling him everything."

"Then why didn't you?"

"For two months James has been preparing for the most important trial of his career."

"You mean to say you're worried about James's career? At a time like this?"

Christy ignored her sister's outburst. "A well-known businessman from Kirkland... You must know Alfred Mulligan. He's the one who does all those crazy television ads. Anyway, he's been charged with cheating on his taxes. The whole case is extremely complicated, and you know as well as I do how messy this kind of thing can get when the federal government is involved." She waited for Taylor to agree with her.

"What's that got to do with anything?"

Christy hated the angry impatience she heard in her sister's voice. It was all too clear that Taylor was upset with her. Christy felt Taylor's disapproval as strongly as a slap, as painfully as a burn. All her life she'd experienced love and approval, especially from her family. It hurt her more than she could bear to feel such overwhelming censure from her only sister.

"You don't understand," Christy cried. "James has been working day and night for several weeks to get ready for this trial. It was scheduled for the first of next month, but he learned this afternoon they've called the case early. He's making the opening statement first thing in the morning."

"I'm afraid I don't understand the importance of all this."

"I don't expect you to. James has worked himself into a frenzy. I've never seen him more upset. So much hangs in the balance for him."

"That's all well and good..."

"He has a chance to win this case, but it's going to be damn difficult," Christy continued, cutting off her sister's protest. "James knows that. Everyone does, but if by some miracle he can pull this off, it could mean a partnership for him."

"Oh, Christy," Taylor said softly, and groaned.

"If I broke off the engagement now, it could ruin everything for him."

"That's James's problem, not yours."

"Maybe it is his problem. I don't know anymore. All I do know is that I can't do this to him. Not on the eve of the most important trial of his career. Not when James has finally been given the chance to prove himself. If anything went wrong, I'd always blame myself."

The silence hummed over the long-distance wire while Taylor considered her words. "What about Cody?" she asked finally. "Have you given any thought to his feelings?"

"Yes." Christy had thought of little else. Never in her life had she asked more of a person than she was of Cody. Another woman had destroyed his trust, and there was little to assure Christy he would want anything to do with her after this.

As painful as it was, as difficult, she found she couldn't humiliate her parents and possibly destroy James's chances with this case.

Even if it meant she lost Cody.

Chapter Nine

Something was wrong. Cody felt it instinctively all the way through to the marrow of his bones. Christy had left two separate messages on his answering machine, and every time he'd played them back, he'd been left with an achy, restless feeling. It wasn't what she'd said, but how she said it. She sounded lighthearted and cheerful, but beneath the bright facade, Cody heard unmistakable confusion and doubt.

He'd tried to phone her back, but to no avail. Unable to sleep, he rose in the early morning hours and drove around the back roads outside of town in an effort to make sense of what was happening. Or not happening.

He couldn't find the answers, not when he wasn't entirely sure he understood the questions.

His greatest fears were about to be realized. Once again it had happened; he'd fallen in love, involved his life with a woman who couldn't be trusted.

Christy isn't Becca, his heart shouted, but Cody had all but given up listening.

The sun had barely crested the hillside as Cody sat in his Cherokee, looking at the valley below, pondering what he should do. If anything. Damn it all, he should never have let this happen. Becca had taught him everything he needed to know about women and love.

Dawn burst over the hillside like a princess bride in all her glory. Golden rays of sunlight splashed against the rugged landscape, and small patches of light lit up the horizon.

Cody released a jagged sigh, reached for the ignition key and started his car. As much as he'd like to turn his back on the entire situation and pretend the past two weeks with Christy hadn't happened, he knew the effort would be futile.

He glanced at his watch, knowing Russ and Taylor would be up and about. He needed to talk.

The light from the kitchen window at the Lazy P glowed in the dissipating darkness as Cody approached the ranch house. He pulled into the yard, turned off the engine and waited until the door opened and Russ appeared on the back porch.

Climbing out of the car, Cody joined his friend.

"I thought that was you," Russ said, opening the door in mute invitation.

Cody removed his hat and set it on the peg while Russ walked over to the coffeepot and automatically poured a mug for his friend.

"Taylor's feeding Eric," Russ said explaining his wife's absence. "She'll be out in a few minutes."

Cody nodded and straddled a high-backed wooden chair.

Russ sat across from him. "Personally I don't think this thing with Christy is as bad as it sounds. Although, to be honest, if I were in your shoes, I don't know what the hell I'd do."

Cody hadn't a clue what his friend was talking about, but he decided not to say anything, hoping Russ would explain without him having to ask.

"How're you holding up?"

"Fine." It was in Cody's mind to drop the charade and ask his friend to explain when Taylor appeared, wearing a soft pink housecoat. Her hair was mussed and fell to the middle of her back. She offered Cody an apologetic smile, and once more he was left to interpret the meaning. His gut was tightening, and he didn't know how much longer he could go on pretending.

"Good morning, Cody," Taylor greeted, helping herself to a cup of coffee. It seemed to Cody her smile conveyed more concern than welcome.

It was all Cody could manage not to leap to his feet and demand someone tell him what the hell was happening.

"I suppose you're here to talk about Christy?" she asked gently. If Russ hadn't said a word, Cody would have guessed something was wrong just from the way Taylor was looking at him—as if she wanted to put her arms around him and weep.

"Christy has been on my mind," he answered brusquely.

"You realize she doesn't have any choice, don't you?" Taylor added. Her eyes, so like Christy's, appealed for him to be open-minded about the situation with her younger sister. "Russ and I've gone round and round about this and—"

"Any choice about what?" Cody demanded, unable to hide the fact he knew next to nothing about the situation. His friends exchanged a surprised look.

"You mean to say Christy wasn't able to get hold of you?"

"No."

"Then you don't know about the engagement party?"

"All I got was two answering machine messages in which she sounds like Mary Sunshine. I knew she wasn't telling me something. I sensed that from the first."

It took a moment for the news to hit him. Engagement party? That meant she was still involved with... If he hadn't already been sitting down, Cody would have needed a chair fast. He'd heard of men who'd had their feet kicked out from under them, but he'd never fully understood the expression until that moment.

"Oh, dear." It was clear from the way Taylor reached for her coffee that she was upset. Her hands trembled, and her gaze avoided meeting his.

Cody transferred his attention to Russ. The rancher looked as uncomfortable as his wife. "What the hell's going on?" Cody demanded.

Once more, husband and wife exchanged glances as if silently deciding between themselves who would do the talking. Apparently Russ presented his wife with the unpleasant task, because she swallowed tightly, then looked at Cody. "My sister's caught in a series of unpleasant circumstances."

"What the hell does that mean?"

"Apparently my mother took the time while Christy was here in Montana to plan an elaborate engagement party. It seems her spirts needed a boost, and my father thought involving her in planning a party would help. Unfortunately in this case he was right. Mom threw herself into the project and arranged for the event of the year, starring Christy and James.''

"You don't mean to tell me she's going through with it?''

"She doesn't have much of a choice. The celebration's scheduled for this evening.''

This second bit of information hit Cody with the same impact as the first. It felt like a punch to the solar plexus. "You've got to be kidding!''

"I wish that was the case,'' Russ inserted, looking annoyed. "My in-laws mean well, and Christy's trapped into going through with this fiasco simply because there isn't time to cancel it now.''

"What about James?'' Cody asked, stiffening at the mention of the other man's name. Every time he thought of the Seattle attorney, he struggled with a wealth of heavy emotion. James Wilkens had far more claim to Christy than he did. They both loved her, but it was James who'd given her an engagement ring. It was James her parents wanted her to marry.

"James is another problem,'' Taylor whispered, and it seemed she grew all the more uneasy.

Cody didn't understand. "You mean he's refusing to release her from the engagement?''

"He doesn't know Christy intends to break it off,'' Russ said without preamble, his voice strained and tight.

Cody would have accepted just about anything more readily than he did this news. Christy had played him for a fool, used him the same way Becca had, for her own selfish purposes.

"She fully intended to tell James everything," Taylor explained heatedly in her sister's defense.

Cody didn't bother to comment, still reeling from this last bit of news.

"When I talked to her, she'd just returned from seeing James. She'd gone to him with the best of intentions, wanting to tell him about you and break off the engagement before it went any farther. More than anything she was hoping the two of them could discuss the engagement party and decide together what could be done."

"She didn't say a word about me to James, did she?" At Taylor's wilted look, Cody decided that was all he needed to know. He stood abruptly, emptied the contents of his mug into the sink and set it so hard on the counter that it was a minor miracle the ceramic mug didn't shatter.

"She couldn't tell him," Taylor cried. "If you love Christy the way you claim, then you'd listen long enough to find out why."

Cody did love Christy, but he didn't know how much more battering his heart and his pride could take. He stood frozen, waiting for Taylor to continue.

"If she told James about you, she might put his entire career in jeopardy." For the next ten minutes Russ and Taylor took turns explaining the situation as best they could.

"Christy doesn't have any choice but to follow through with this farce of a party, don't you see?"

Taylor did an admirable job of presenting her sister's case. Cody would grant her that much.

She kept her pleading eyes focused on him. "If it had been up to her, she would have ended the engagement five minutes after she arrived home."

Cody didn't respond, although it was apparent his friends were waiting for him to say something. Anything.

"You've got to appreciate the situation Christy's in," Taylor went on. "What would you have done had the circumstances been reversed?"

Cody would have liked to think he had all the answers. But he didn't. What could he do? He closed his eyes to ponder the situation.

Honest to God, he just didn't know.

"Oh, sweetheart!" Christy's mother exclaimed, stepping back to examine the effect of the full-length layered blue dress. She pressed her fingertips to her lips and blinked back ready tears. "You look like an angel. Eric, come and see."

Eric Manning, dressed in a white tuxedo with a pale blue cummerbund the same shade of blue as Christy's dress, gingerly stepped into the living room. He eyed his youngest daughter and nodded approvingly. "You make an old man proud," he said with a warm, encompassing smile.

"I don't know when you've ever looked more lovely," her mother added.

Christy managed a smile. She hadn't a clue how she was going to make it through this party. She might be able to fool her parents, but surely someone would notice. Rich would. Of her three brothers, she'd always been closest to Rich. He'd take one look at her and immediately guess something was very wrong.

Not that it would make any difference. She would stand before family and friends and pretend to be madly in love with James, pretend to be an eager bride in waiting. But the only thing Christy was eager for at the moment was to put this evening behind her.

"I'd like to propose a toast to the happy couple, my sister Christy and the one love of her life, James Wilkens." Rich Manning raised his champagne glass to the couple.

Christy grinned at her brother and battled back the urge to empty her champagne glass over his head. Of all the guests, she had expected him to realize how miserable she was. Instead, he unwittingly heaped salt upon her tender wounds.

A smiling sea of faces nodded appreciatively at her brother's words before the party-goers sipped the vintage champagne. The round of toasts had been going on for several minutes. Christy wasn't sure how much more of this she could endure.

Her father had proposed the first toast, followed by her uncles and all three of her brothers. Each seemed to add something more to the list of glad tidings they wished to bestow on James and his bride-to-be.

Christy swallowed another sip of her champagne as her fiancé stood at her side, tall and debonair. He was a refined, quiet man, gentle of nature, dedicated and kind.

Christy could barely look at him without being overwhelmed with crushing guilt. They'd spent two hours in each other's company, and neither of them had spoken more than a handful of sentences.

In retrospect Christy wondered how she could possibly have agreed to spend the rest of her life with James. He was wonderful, but it was painfully obvious they were mismatched.

Hoping she wasn't being conspicuous, Christy scanned the gathering, wondering if it were possible for anyone to have read her thoughts. Not that it would do any good.

"Would you like something to eat?" James asked, glancing toward the linen-draped tables where several trays of hors d'oeuvres lay waiting.

Christy shook her head, confident she wouldn't be able to hold down a single bite. "Nothing for me, thanks. What about you?"

"I'm fine," James answered, and briefly shook his head.

The music started, and a handful of couples were making their way to the gleaming wooden floor. "I've always been terrible at this sort of thing," James confessed, reaching for Christy's hand. "But I suppose it's expected of us."

Christy nodded, wanting nothing more than to escape. A path was cleared as James led the way to the dance floor and slipped his arm around her waist, being careful to maintain a respectable distance between them. The music was slow and melodious, a love ballad, the words of which seemed to ridicule her more than anything that had preceded the dancing.

James smiled softly into Christy's eyes as they moved across the floor. Soon the other couples joined them.

Her fiancé seemed to relax a little more now that they weren't the only two on the floor. For that matter so did Christy. "I'm sorry I haven't been myself this evening," James murmured regretfully.

Christy was ashamed to admit she hadn't noticed. Her whole attention had been focused on simply getting through this ordeal.

"The Mulligan case is going to take up a good portion of my time over the next couple of weeks. I know it's a lot to ask, but I can only hope you'll be patient with me."

Christy was horrified to realize she'd forgotten all about the trial and how important it was to him. "Oh, James, I'm so sorry. I didn't even ask how everything went this morning."

"Not as good as I'd hoped," he mumbled under his breath.

For James to admit that much spoke volumes. "I understand if you're going to be terribly busy. In fact, it might work for the best. You see, I met someone—" She wasn't allowed to finish.

"I knew you'd be understanding," he said, cutting her off. He smiled gently and settled his chin at the crown of her head. "You always have been."

"You, too," she whispered sarcastically, but James didn't seem to notice.

Closing her eyes, she tried to pretend it was Cody's arms around her. It was the only way she was going to be able to continue this farce. Keeping his image in her mind gave her a sense of purpose, a means of enduring this disastrous night.

After a respectable number of dances, James led the way off the floor. Until then Christy hadn't noticed how tired and defeated he looked. Several family members insisted upon dances with her. Christy found herself on the floor with a number of uncles, her brothers and longtime family friends.

James was doing his duty, as well, keeping the women from both families occupied. She did notice that he managed to do so without dancing with them, however, and found herself amused by how he cleverly avoided doing so.

It wasn't until the end of the evening, just when Christy was convinced she would survive, that her Aunt Lois, her mother's youngest sister, asked the impossible. "When's the date for the wedding?"

It seemed as if the whole room went silent. The music ceased, and everyone turned to stare at Christy and James. They were sitting together in a long row of folding chairs set against the wall. It was the first time that evening that they'd sat down.

Christy felt like a cornered animal. The cracker in her mouth seemed to go down her throat whole.

"You don't have an engagement party without letting those you love know when you're planning the wedding," her Aunt Lois continued.

James glanced at Christy. "We haven't had a chance to discuss a date, have we, darling?"

"No," Christy managed. It wouldn't look good for her to announce she was counting the days until she could break off the engagement. If she was going to discuss a wedding date with anyone, it would be with Cody. But he hadn't asked her, and after he learned about this evening, Christy doubted he'd ever have anything to do with her again.

"Springtime is always a lovely time of year for a wedding." Aunt Lois stood directly in front of her, waving her arms, demanding the attention of Christy and everyone else. "George and I were married in May, and the flowers were gorgeous." Pressing her gloved hands together, she released a slow sigh of remembered happiness.

"But May's several months from now. Why, it's almost a year away," Elizabeth Manning objected loudly, walking all the way across the dance floor to join in this all-important discussion. "Why wait so long? I was thinking more along the lines of November."

"November?" Christy echoed.

"The leaves are always so pretty then. You know how I love orange, brown and yellow," she said, looking at her daughter.

Already Christy could see her mother's mind working, plotting and planning. She'd enjoyed making the arrangements for the engagement party so much that she could barely wait to get her fingers into all the pomp and ceremony of a formal wedding.

"With your dark coloring, Christy, an autumn theme would be perfect."

"Personally I favor a December wedding," Eric Manning shouted. He'd obviously had more than his share of champagne.

"December?" Elizabeth shrieked, shaking her head. "Never."

"All right," Eric countered smoothly. "Let's ask Christy and James which date they prefer. This is, after all, their wedding."

"Ah," Christy couldn't think. Her mind froze along with her hands, which were raised halfway to her mouth, her fingers clenching a delicate artichoke canapé. In a panic she looked at James, her eyes wide in speechless appeal. If ever she needed rescuing, it was now.

"What do you say, sweetheart?" her mother pressed.

By some miracle Christy managed to lower the cracker to her plate. "I . . . I haven't given the matter much thought."

"When George and I decided to marry, we couldn't do it fast enough," Aunt Lois informed the group.

"November," James said decisively. "Your aunt's right. There's no need to put off the wedding, not when we're so much in love."

"We don't have to decide *now*, do we?" Christy asked softly. "Not when you're so busy with the Mulligan case."

His hand gently patted hers. "This trial will be over soon enough, and I've been selfish to the extreme not to consider your feelings. Naturally you and your mother will want to start making all the necessary arrangements."

"November would be perfect." Elizabeth Manning opened her purse and withdrew a small appointment calendar. "Let's pick the date right now. How does the twelfth sound?"

Once more Christy found herself speechless. "Ah..."

"The twelfth sounds grand," James claimed triumphantly, and lightly pressed his lips to Christy's cheek. "Isn't that right, darling?"

The whole world came to an abrupt halt, awaiting Christy's reply. The walls seemed to be falling in around her, trapping her with steel claws.

"Christy?" her mother probed, eyeing her curiously. "November 12 sounds like a beautiful day for a wedding, don't you agree?"

Cody slowly patrolled the deserted streets of Cougar Point, but his mind wasn't on his job. The biggest crime wave of the century could have happened before his very eyes, and Cody doubted he would have recognized what was going on.

How could he? The only reason he'd agreed to take this shift was in an effort to forget that Christy was with James this evening.

While Cody dutifully served his constituents, Christy was sipping champagne with her attorney fiancé. No doubt his diamond was firmly placed on her ring finger and she was having the time of her life.

The thought had a curious effect on him.

It hurt.

The pain was as real as anything he'd ever endured. Except that it hurt more. There wasn't a damn thing he could do to alter the chain of events that had led Christy into this predicament. Apparently there was damn little she could do, either.

Knowing that should have eased his apprehensions, but it didn't. He tried to remind himself that the woman he loved would do everything within her power not to hurt others, even if it meant hurting herself. But Christy wasn't the only one suffering.

Cody felt as if he'd been wounded in the line of duty. A casualty of circumstance.

It was late when Cody rolled into the station—after eleven. He climbed out of the patrol car and noted Russ's pickup truck was parked out front. Frowning, he made his way into the station.

Russ Palmer unfolded his long legs and stood. "It's about time you got here."

"Problems?"

Russ nodded. "A few. I thought it might be a good idea if we talked."

The anxiety that had been following him around like a tide of bad luck grew more intense. "I'll meet you in ten minutes."

Since the bowling alley was the only restaurant in town that stayed open this late, Cody didn't need to mention where they'd meet.

Russ was already in the booth, holding on to a white ceramic mug when Cody walked inside. Cody slid into the booth, wondering how his best friend had known to pick the same booth he'd sat in with Christy. He'd been in love with her then and hadn't even known it.

"What's so all-fired important to bring you out this time of night?" Cody asked.

"Taylor."

That didn't explain a hell of a lot.

The cook brought out a second mug for Cody and promptly returned to the kitchen. Russ's gaze followed the other man. Cody didn't need a crystal ball to realize something more had gone wrong and Russ was about to tell him about it.

"What did Christy do now? Run off with Gypsies? Marry the garbageman?"

"Worse."

"I suppose this has to do with the engagement party."

Once more Russ nodded. "Apparently no one guessed her real feelings. It seems everyone was too concerned about how much liquor made it into the punch bowl to ask Christy how she felt about the whole thing."

"I should be grateful for that?"

"No," Russ answered starkly. "She went through the evening like a real trooper. She loves her family, and she did this for their sake, but she didn't like it."

"She's not the only one."

"I can well imagine," Russ said with a sympathetic sigh. "God knows how I'd feel in like circumstances."

"Hell, I don't know what to do anymore." Cody rubbed a hand down his face, lost in a churning caldron of doubt. "Tell me what happened. I can deal with that better than not knowing."

Russ seemed lost, unsure where to begin.

"Just spit it out," Cody urged. By everything that was right, he should forget he'd ever met Christy Manning.

"She's sick. Apparently she started throwing up at the party itself. Taylor talked to her and said Christy's in pretty rough shape."

For all his effort to portray a disinterested party, Cody's heart raced to the news as though it had been struck with a sledgehammer. "What's wrong?"

"It's not what you think."

"If she's in as rough shape as you say, then why the hell didn't she contact me?"

"She's been trying to reach you for two days."

"I've been busy. Hell, what was I supposed to do? Phone her and suggest she enjoy her engagement party? I have some pride left, and frankly I'm holding on to it."

"She needs to talk to you. Call her."

Cody shrugged.

"If you've been avoiding her, don't. She doesn't deserve this. Not now."

"I've tried phoning," Cody confessed, as if admitting to a shortcoming in his character. "She's never there."

"You didn't leave a message?"

"No," he answered reluctantly. What was there to say over a machine that would help their situation? As far as he could see, nothing.

"She's at her apartment now. Take my advice and put each other out of this misery. Talk to her."

* * *

Ten minutes later Cody unlocked his front door and walked into his living room. The phone seemed to glare at him in the dark like a fluorescent light. He didn't know who the hell he was trying to kid. He was so hungry for the sound of Christy's voice, he was nearly faint with malnutrition.

It was necessary to fortify himself before he dialed the Seattle number. He convinced himself he was the injured party and that if anyone needed reassurances, it was he.

Christy gave him all the encouragement he needed by answering even before the first ring had finished sounding.

"Cody?" Her sweet voice caught on his name before he had a chance to speak.

"Hello, Christy," he said in a voice that would have pleased Joe Friday of *Dragnet* fame. He sounded poised, cool, distant.

"Thank you for calling me."

"You're welcome." How cold and stiff that sounded, even though talking to her was having exactly the opposite effect on him.

"Did Taylor tell you?"

"Tell me what?"

"About what happened at the party?"

"No." There was more? "Russ came into town and asked me to contact you. He eluded to something but never said what. Go ahead and tell me."

The slight hesitation that followed answered that question. "I . . . it isn't easy."

"Damn it, Christy, what the hell's going on now?" A list of possibilities did little to put him at ease.

"I want to be honest with you," she said, her voice shaking. "I..." She paused, and Cody could hear her drag a deep breath through her lungs as if fortifying herself. "Something happened at the party tonight...something I never intended."

Cody would have liked to have come off as nonchalant, but it was impossible. He expelled his breath, trying to think of what she might have done that would have been bad enough for him to stop loving her.

Nothing. She could do nothing. Even if she were to inform him she'd given into the pressure and married James that very night, it wouldn't be enough to make him stop loving her.

"November 12," she whispered.

"I beg your pardon?" She'd gone from guessing games to mind puzzles.

"The wedding with James is set for November 12."

Chapter Ten

Christy rolled over and glanced at the illuminated dial of her clock radio. It was 10:00 a.m.

This was supposed to be her first day back at the office, and she'd been forced to phone in sick. A flu bug was what she'd told Marcia, the office manager, who was sympathetic enough to suggest Christy stay home so as not to spread the germ. But it wasn't the flu that was making her ill.

It was something else entirely. Christy was heartsick, afraid she'd lost Cody forever. She was caught in a trap doing what was right for everyone but herself.

Now she was wide awake, and the day stretched before her like a millennium. She could occupy herself with mindless game shows on television, but that would only take an hour or more. Reading would help pass the time. She might even give some thought to phoning Cody.

No.

That was out of the question. Cody didn't want to talk to her, not anymore. She'd said everything she could to make him understand her predicament two nights earlier. Everything had gone reasonably well until she'd voluntarily told him she'd been forced into setting a date for the wedding.

An unexpected sob tore through her throat, and fresh tears dampened her eyes. She'd done much weeping over the past couple of days. Damp, crumbled tissues formed a semicircle across the top of her bedspread where she'd carelessly discarded them.

She loved Cody, and nothing she'd been able to say had convinced him of that truth. Cody, being a sheriff, saw everything in terms of black and white. Either she had agreed to the wedding date or she hadn't. Unfortunately Christy had sanctioned November 12, more or less, when pressured. As soon as she confessed as much, her telephone conversation with Cody had ended abruptly.

She'd pleaded with Cody for understanding, said everything she knew to assure him she would never willingly marry James, but it hadn't helped. They'd hung up with Cody promising to contact her after he'd had some time to think matters through.

Nearly thirty-four hours had passed. Surely he'd had adequate opportunity to come to some kind of decision.

The doorbell chimed, and sniffling, Christy reached for another tissue. She noisily blew her nose before tossing aside her covers and climbing out of bed. Whoever it was, she fully intended to send them away. She was in no mood for company.

With the way her luck was running, it was probably her mother wanting to discuss color schemes for the bridesmaids' dresses. If her car hadn't been parked directly in front of her door, she wouldn't even bother answering.

"Who is it?" she asked, squinting through the peephole and seeing no one.

"Cody Franklin."

"Cody... oh, Cody." Christy hurriedly threw open the door. Her breasts were heaving as though she'd just finished an aerobic workout. For one wild second she did nothing but stare into his wonderful face, convinced he was a figment of her imagination. Before another instant could mark time, she launched herself into his arms.

Cody dropped the suitcase, gripping her around the waist with both arms. He hauled her to him with joyful abandon. Their mouths met in a kiss so fierce, it threatened to knock her off balance and steal her breath. He held her as if he were starving for the taste of her, and meant to make up for every moment of every day they'd been apart.

Christy's arms came up and encircled his neck, her mouth parting with giddy abandon, her tongue finding his, touching, stroking, warring in an agony of need.

With a shudder Cody tore his mouth away from hers and spread a wildfire of kisses over each delicate feature of her face. His arms held her tightly around the waist, and her feet dangled several inches off the ground as his chest heaved in several deep breaths.

Weeping for joy, Christy pressed her head against his shoulder, feeling completely at ease for the first time since she'd left Montana. She was in Cody's arms. Nothing could ever hurt her again.

"I think it might be a good idea if we went inside," he whispered.

Christy nodded. Slowly he released her, and she slid down his front, aware of every male nuance of this man, loving him beyond reason.

"How'd you get here?" she asked, searching the parking lot for signs of his Cherokee.

"I flew," he explained as his hand stroked the tumbling mass of curls away from her face. "I couldn't leave matters between us the way they were. At least not without us talking this out face-to-face. I took three days' vacation, hoping we could put an end to his craziness."

Christy was looking for the same thing. She took hold of his wrist and pulled him inside her small apartment. She closed the door and then turned to face him, her hands pressed behind her. One look at him and she felt so discouraged.

From the moment she'd arrived in Seattle, she'd stood alone against what seemed like overwhelming forces. Her mother needed her. James needed her. Everyone wanted a part of her until she felt as if she were being torn in two.

"How . . . how'd you know I was home?" she asked once her mind had cleared enough to properly process her thoughts. That he'd arrive on her doorstep was too much of a coincidence.

"I phoned the law firm from the airport. They told me you were out with the flu."

Christy couldn't believe what she was hearing. Cody had phoned her at the office!

"You disapprove?" His eyes bored into her, demanding an answer.

"No." But her heart was thumping so loud it sounded like a steam engine inside her chest. It wasn't likely anyone had given his inquiry a second thought. Even if they had, she wouldn't be around to answer their questions.

"But the fact I'd talked to someone who knew you and James gave you cause for concern, didn't it?" He started to pace her compact living room. Four long strides covered the entire length of it. He buried one hand in his back pocket while the other was massaging the muscles at his nape as if to work out the tightness. "You're so afraid your precious James is going to find out about me."

"That's not true," she denied vehemently. Too late, Christy realized she probably was the most pathetic sight he'd ever seen.

Her eyes were red and swollen, and she hadn't even bothered to get dressed. The five-year-old pajamas she was wearing were as sexy as dirty dishes. Not that any of this seemed to bother Cody, who was apparently far more interested in arguing with her than ravishing her.

In her emotionally fragile condition Christy was much too weak to withstand a heated verbal exchange. Everyone was coming at her with advice. Taylor knew without a doubt what would be best. Russ, too. But no one was willing to listen to her. No one understood what she was suffering. It was all fine and dandy to dish out advice when a thousand miles separated everyone from the situation.

She was the one on the front line. She was the one who'd have to face her parents. She seemed to be the one who appreciated the long years of hard work that had led James to this point in his career. She couldn't, wouldn't, ruin his chances now.

If Cody Franklin honestly expected her to buy their happiness at the expense of another, then he didn't really know her at all.

He turned abruptly to face her. Boldly she met the piercing quality of his eyes, staring down the hot accusation she felt in him.

He met her glare, and Christy felt his anger start to dissolve, replaced with doubt and pain. Defeated, he expelled a harsh breath. His shoulders sagged. "Forget I ever mentioned James. I didn't come here to fight about him."

"Then why did you come?"

He didn't seem to have the answer, or if he did, he wasn't willing to supply it just yet. He pulled his gaze away from her and plowed his fingers through his thick hair. "To talk some sense into you and put an end to this before we both go insane."

How Christy wished it were that simple.

"This situation isn't as complicated as you're making it. Either you're serious about loving me or you aren't. It should be a simple matter of setting the record straight, but—"

"I do love you."

"Then why are you wearing another man's ring?" he demanded. He stalked toward her and pulled her hand out from behind her back. His eyes narrowed as he found her ring finger bare.

"I've only worn James's diamond once. The night of the engagement party," she explained, surprised by how strained her voice sounded. "I removed it the minute I walked in the door and haven't put it on since."

Cody's large, callused hand curled over her fingers as he shut his eyes. The muscles in his jaw clenched. Then, moving slowly, as though hypnotized, he lowered his mouth to hers. His touch was gentle, as soft as lamb-skin.

Her lips trembled under his and parted slightly as his hot, moist tongue made lazy circles around the seam of her lips.

Christy closed her eyes as hard as she could, wanting to shut out the harsh realities between them. She longed to block out everything, except the man who was holding her so gently, and loving her so tenderly.

She trembled, needing his strength and comfort more than she'd needed anything in her life. Snuggling closer, she reached up, standing on tiptoe so the softness of her breasts nuzzled the hard wall of his chest. Her tongue boldly met his as the kiss deepened.

Cody's hands cupped her buttocks, lifting her slightly. She moved against him shamelessly, growing more bold and excited by his passionate response. She felt intoxicated to realize how much he wanted her. Her hands were trembling as she blindly pulled his shirt lose from his waistband. Not wanting to take the trouble to unfasten the buttons, she lifted the shirt and flattened her hands against his heaving chest, luxuriating in the feel of his hot skin beneath her palms. He felt incredibly strong, incredibly male. His skin was fever-hot, the muscles of his stomach hard and smooth. She hesitated for an instant, then slid her hand past his waistline, inching her fingers across his tightening abdomen.

"Christy...no," he groaned.

"Don't tell me you're going to argue with me."

"I'm going to argue with you."

"Why?" The lone word was soft and filled with unspoken need. Slowly she rotated her hips against him.

"In the name of heaven, Christy...stop."

"No." She branded his bottom lip with the tip of her tongue, then caught it between her teeth and sucked lightly, pulling it into her mouth. Their tongues circled each other's in a ravenous, carnal kiss.

"Tell me to stop and I will."

It didn't seem possible to Christy that anything could feel this wonderful. Instinct directed her actions, and after taking several oxygen-hungry breaths, she lowered her mouth to the throbbing hollow of his strong neck.

His pulse was steady and strong. The feel of it against her mouth excited her in ways she was only beginning to understand.

"Christy?"

She ignored the plea she heard in his voice, and kissed his throat a second time, excited by his warmth, reveling in his salty taste. Her breasts continued to knead his chest, her nipples had puckered, and every swirl of her hips scraped against his muscular strength, creating a whole realm of dizzying sensations.

This was all so new to her. She'd never been so bold with a man. She'd never abandoned herself to such a wealth of sexual feelings. Loving Cody made everything right.

Cody was her reward.

Just when she'd started to peel off her pajama top and bare her breasts, Cody's hands closed forcefully around her hips, pushing her several inches away. "Dear sweet heaven..." His voice was little more than a hoarse whisper. "This has got to end...right now before..."

"Why? Doesn't it feel as good to you?"

"Oh, Christy, yes. Too damn good." He ground out the words through clenched teeth and let his arms fall away from her. "We can't do this. Not with the way things are between us."

Feeling completely and totally brazen, Christy flattened her hand over the evidence of his desire and sighed longingly at the strength, heat and power beneath her fingertips. "I'd say matters between us were as solid as they can get."

"We need to talk," he growled, but Christy had the feeling the battle he was raging was with himself.

"Isn't 'I love you' enough talk?" Although he struggled to hold her at bay, Christy spread nibbling kisses at the curve of his neck, loving the control she felt over him. She wanted him so much, her body felt as if it would melt if he didn't make love to her soon.

Cody released a sharp, ragged sigh and abruptly propelled himself away from her. He moved so fast and so unexpectedly that Christy nearly stumbled forward. Bewildered, she caught herself just in time.

By then Cody had put the full distance of the living room between them. "In case it's slipped your mind, I'd like to remind you, you're an engaged woman."

The only time she was allowed to forget that was when Cody was holding and kissing her. She blinked back her pain. For him to throw the details of this farce of an engagement into her face now was cruel and unusual punishment.

"If you flew all those miles to remind me of that, then you made a wasted trip." Humiliation tainted her cheeks a hot shade of pink. It was all she could do not to cover her face with both hands and turn away from him.

In his arms she'd been willing to sacrifice everything—her pride, her self-respect and twenty odd years of strict moral upbringing.

And he was rejecting her.

For several minutes neither of them spoke. It was as if they both required time to compose themselves. Cody continued pacing, while Christy stood rooted, leaning against the front door, requiring its strength to hold her upright. It was something of a shock to discover how badly she was trembling.

"I need to ask you to do something," Cody said crisply, as if whatever he was about to say didn't involve him emotionally in any way.

"All right."

"Break the engagement to James." His dark eyes cut into her with sharp, unquestioning demand. Christy could tell by the way he held himself, by the way he paced with precise steps, that he was struggling to remain as objective as possible.

"Of course. You know I will the very first moment I can—"

"I want you to do it now. Today."

Full of regret and anguish, Christy closed her eyes in an effort to hide. This problem with James had tormented her from the moment she arrived home and talked to him. Surely Cody realized she didn't want to stay engaged to another man.

"Christy?"

"I . . . can't break it off. Not now. You know that. James has been working for three months getting ready for this trial. He was as prepared as any attorney could be, and yet one thing after another has gone wrong for him. I can't add to his troubles by—"

"We have no business seeing each other," Cody interrupted. "We didn't when you were in Montana, and we have even less of an excuse now that you're home."

"But I love you."

Her words fell into a weighted silence. Cody didn't answer for so long that she began to worry. His expression told her nothing of his thoughts.

"Love doesn't make everything right," he said, his eyes darkening with bitterness. "I wish to God it did, but the way we feel about each other doesn't alter one damn thing. You're promised to another man, and that's all there is to it."

"But...Cody."

"Not only do you have his ring, you've got a wedding date set."

"I explained all that," she whispered, feeling utterly defenseless.

"At the moment, though, your engagement to James is the least of our troubles."

Christy blinked, not sure she understood what he was saying.

"We're so damn hot for each other, we're both about to explode."

"I know," she whispered, swallowing her share of the blame for the shameless way she'd made him want her. At the shameless way she'd wanted him.

"There's something you don't seem to understand," Cody said, frowning heavily. "I'm a man of honor, a man of my word..."

It hurt that he would doubt she recognized that. "I couldn't love you as much as I do without knowing the kind of man you are."

"Then you must realize how continuing what's between us makes me feel."

She stared over at him, barely able to believe she'd been so stupid not to think of her engagement in those terms. Cody wasn't being possessive or jealous. It wasn't his pride that was injured or his healthy ego. It was a sense of fair play. A matter of honesty.

He rubbed a hand down his face and slowly shook his head. "For both our sakes, I wish I were different. I'd like nothing better than to steal a few days away with you, hold you, kiss you. More than anything else in this world I want to make love to you, but I can't allow that to happen."

Christy wanted all those things, as well.

"The fact you were committed to James bothered the hell out of me when you were staying with Russ and Taylor. The fact you didn't want to break the engagement over the phone wasn't unreasonable and I understood as best I could."

Christy now wished she'd put an end to everything then. How much simpler her life would be.

"It wasn't easy to keep my hands off you then, and it's a hell of a lot more difficult now." His voice was incredibly tight, and he didn't slacken his stride as he continued pacing the confines of her compact living room. "I can't play this game with you any longer. Either you break it off with James, right now, today, or it's over. I'll fly back to Montana and this will be the last of it."

Christy felt as if the entire ceiling had come crashing down on her head. She might have withstood the impact far more easily than she did his decree.

"The last of it?" she repeated, struggling to keep her voice from pitching and heaving.

"Christy, for the love of God, look at it from my point of view."

"I am. All I'm asking for... all I need is for you to be a little more patient. The trial will be over soon."

"I've been more than patient already."

"But it'll only be for a little while longer. I swear to you. I'll break it off with James at the first opportunity. But I can't do it now." The urgency in her voice echoed off the walls and came back to haunt her.

Once again her words fell into a heavy void and she was left to wonder at his thoughts. "Cody...please," she whispered when she couldn't tolerate the silence any longer.

He pivoted sharply. "I know you. You're warm and loving, and it goes against that soft heart of yours to disturb a fly."

If he understood her so well, then surely he'd be willing to be patient just a little while longer. She was about to say something along those lines when he added, "You've allowed your parents to manipulate you all your life."

"That's not true," she cried, wanting to defend herself, angry that he would even suggest something like that.

"They handpicked a husband for you, and you went along with it without a pause."

Some of the starch went out of her shoulders, but her indignation had yet to cool.

"You didn't love James then and you don't love him now, or so you claim."

"I love you," she cried. "How many times do I have to say it?"

"Yet when James offered you an engagement ring, you accepted his proposal."

"I...I..." The flag of her outrage went limp for lack of an argument. Everything he said was true, but it had happened before she'd met Cody.

"You're so eager to take care of everyone else you're willing to sacrifice your own happiness."

"All I need is a few more days, just until this trial..." She didn't finish, realizing nothing she said was going to change his mind.

"I don't know what's going to happen between you, your attorney friend and your parents. Frankly I have a strong suspicion that you're going to wake up one fine morning married to dear old James and not realize how it happened."

"That's utterly ridiculous." She folded her arms around her middle to ward off an unexpected chill. "I swear to you that will never happen."

"You swore to me you were going to break the engagement when you arrived back in Seattle, too. Remember?"

His dark eyes challenged her to deny it. She couldn't, but he wasn't fighting fair. He met her rock-hard stare, but it was Christy who looked away first, Christy whose gaze flickered under the force of the truth.

"But how could I have known about the engagement party?" she queried weakly. Then, gaining conviction, she glared at him. "You're not being fair. To even suggest I'd go ahead with the wedding is—" she searched for the right word "—ludicrous."

"Is it really?"

"Of course it is. You make me sound like some weak-willed... I can't imagine why you'd want to have anything to do with me if that's the way you feel."

"I love you, Christy, and it's going to hurt like hell to walk away from you. My request isn't an unreasonable one, although I know you don't agree with that."

She edged her way to the door, leaning against the frame as if doing so would be enough to stop him. "You can't ask me to make that kind of decision. Not right this minute. I need time to think everything through carefully.'' In the back of her mind she was desperately praying the Mulligan case would be thrown out of court that afternoon and this whole regrettable affair could be laid to rest.

She might win the lottery, too, but she couldn't count on it.

"Is the decision that difficult?" Cody asked, frowning. "That on its own says something, whether you're willing to admit it or not."

Christy shut her eyes and took a deep breath. The man she loved, her entire future, was about to walk out the door, and she knew of no way to stop him short of destroying another.

Straightening, she glared across the room at Cody. "I don't know what's right anymore," she cried defiantly. "How can I? All everyone does is make demands of me. First it's Mom and then James and now...you."

Then she did the most incredible thing. Christy Manning started weeping. Her shoulders shook and her head bobbed violently. The tips of her fingers covered her mouth as she struggled to hold a week's worth of heartache at bay.

She heard Cody mutter a swear word, which was so unlike him. If he was confused, it was nothing to what she was feeling. The tears, the emotion, were as much of a surprise to her as they were to him.

"Christy, please, I can't bear to see you cry," he whispered hoarsely.

He could break her heart, but he couldn't stand to see her weep. Christy found the thought almost laughable.

Cody moved across the room and gently took her into his arms. His hands stroked the tumbled hair away from her brow. With him she felt secure. With him she felt warm and protected. She buried her face in the hollow of his neck as the emotion worked through her. He held her close until she was able to draw in a deep, shaky breath. Christy could feel her control gently slipping back into place.

Still Cody held her, his hands caressing her back in soothing, gentle ways. For the longest time he said nothing. He continued holding her close, and after several moments Christy became aware of how wonderfully intimate their position was.

She sighed longingly and tested her discovery by tenderly licking the strong cord of his neck. A moment passed in which she waited for him to protest, or gently ease himself away from her.

Experiencing a small sense of triumph when he didn't, she leisurely investigated the warm, tantalizing skin, making slow, moist circles over the hollow of his throat.

"Kiss me," she whispered. "Oh, please, Cody, just kiss me. I'll be all right if you'll do that."

He didn't immediately comply with her request. In fact, he seemed inclined to ignore her, as if nothing would be proved, nothing would be solved by kissing. Perhaps he was right, but Christy was having a difficult time discerning what was right and what was wrong.

He froze when she planted her hands on each side of his strong face, working her mouth up his jawline, moistly sliding her lips and her tongue over his chin until their mouths were joined.

Cody groaned like a man trapped in a torture chamber, sucking in his breath as her tongue found and mated with his. He moaned anew when she slanted her mouth over his and kissed him with all the hunger and love in her sensitive heart.

His hands were trembling as he started to remove her pajama top. The tiny fasteners soon frustrated him, and in his haste the buttons popped. He removed the top, moving it halfway down her shoulders, imprisoning her arms. His mouth reluctantly left hers and slid down the side of her neck, leaving a damp line. His descent continued on a straight path over her collarbone until he located her lush breasts. He paused and lapped the pulsing buds several times each before greedily latching onto her. He suckled one and then the other, paying equal attention to both.

Christy threw back her head as he administered his loving attention. Lost in a thick fog of passion, she squirmed and twisted until Cody lowered his hands to her buttocks. His fingers dug into her derrière, lifting her slightly as he ground his hips against her softness, seemingly desperate to satisfy the raging fires of their passion. Christy was lost in the wonder of her own desire, of her own incredible need.

With a harsh groan Cody freed her. It seemed for one wild moment that he meant to break away from her. She couldn't allow that, and in an effort to hold him she locked her arms around his neck. Moaning, he clamped his mouth over hers in a kiss so fiery, it was a miracle they both didn't burst into flames.

"Christy... In the name of God..." He tore his mouth from her. It seemed as if his whole body was shaking as he inhaled. "See what I mean?"

"Yes," she whispered, and softly kissed his brow.

"I don't know what the hell we're going to do." When he composed himself, he broke away from her and walked over to her sofa. He sat on the edge of the cushion, braced his elbows against his knees and wiped his hands down his face two or three times. "I'm not strong enough to walk away from you. I thought I could."

"I won't let you go." She sat next to him, pressed her forehead to his shoulder and sighed bitterly. "I love you so damn much.... I'd give anything I could if it were possible to marry you today."

Cody went stock-still. "What did you just say?"

Chapter Eleven

"I won't let you go, Cody. I can't," Christy repeated.

"Not that," he said, bolting to his feet. He started pacing again, and when she didn't immediately continue, he added, "It was after that."

She frowned, not understanding. "I love you?"

"Not that, either. It's the part about marrying me today if it were possible."

"I would." She didn't feel the least bit hesitation in suggesting as much. Almost from the first day she'd met the newly elected Custer County sheriff, she'd known she was going to love him all the days of her life.

"Will you marry me, Christy?" His expression was so open and warm and sincere that she felt tears sting the back of her eyes.

"Oh, yes," she whispered. She would probably be the only woman in the world engaged to two men at the same time, but that couldn't be helped.

"I mean now."

"Now?" She wasn't sure she followed his line of thinking.

"I'd like us to be married this afternoon."

Her heart responded with a quick, wistful beat, but Christy didn't know how a wedding, that day, would be possible.

"It . . . it may be different in Montana, but Washington State has a three-day waiting period after we apply for the license."

A slow smile eased up the corners of his mouth. "Idaho doesn't."

Still Christy was having a difficult time understanding. "That may be, but Idaho's over 350 miles from here. If you're only going to be in Seattle three days, we'll end up spending two of those on the road."

"That's easily fixed. I'll rent a plane." He paused and smiled a breathtaking smile that was so appealing, she thought she would die a slow death if he didn't make love to her soon. "Am I going too fast for you?"

"No," she rushed to assure him, although her mind was abuzz. "It's just that I'm having a little trouble understanding. What about James?" She hated mentioning fiancé number one, but she had to be certain they were doing the right thing for the right reasons.

"What about him?"

"Will I . . . do I have to tell him about the wedding? I mean, it won't make much of a difference if he learns I've married you a couple of days from now or even until next week, does it? The only reason I'm suggesting I delay telling him is because of the trial."

Some of the happy excitement left Cody's eyes. "I'll leave that part up to you. As far as James is concerned, I don't know what's right or wrong anymore. All I know is that I love you more than I thought it was possible to love any woman. It scares the living hell out of me to think I could lose you."

"There isn't the slightest chance of that."

His smile was sad as he shook his head. "I meant what I said earlier about fearing you'd end up married to James. I've had nightmares about it, wondering if I'd get a call in the middle of the night. I've dreamed you phoned to explain how everything got out of your control and you'd married James before you could think of a way to stop the ceremony."

"I would never allow such a thing."

He gave her a distrusting look, cocking both of his thick brows. Although it injured her pride to admit it, Christy could well appreciate Cody's concern. The circumstances she found herself in were unbelievable.

"I feel a whole lot better making damn sure that couldn't happen." The warmth of his look removed the sting his words might have inflicted. "I learned a long time ago to cover all my bases. Us marrying like this may not be the best thing, but we're making a commitment to each other, and heaven help me for being so weak, but I need that."

Heaven help him! Christy felt herself go soft on the inside. She wanted him with a fierce hunger that she was only now beginning to understand. "Oh, Cody, I love you so much."

"Good," he said, his voice slightly husky, "because you're about to become my wife."

He smiled, completely disarming her. If Christy had a single argument, which she didn't, one of those devastating smiles of his would have settled it.

"How soon can you be ready?"

"An hour?"

"Good, I'll check the phone book and make the arrangements while you dress." He captured her hands and helped her to her feet, pausing long enough to plant a sweet kiss on her unsuspecting lips.

In something of a daze Christy walked into her bedroom and searched through her closets for something special enough for her own wedding. Smiling to herself, she traipsed to the doorway of her bedroom and leaned idly against the jamb. "The whole thing's off. I don't have anything decent to wear," she said, teasing him.

Cody sat at her kitchen table, leafing through the impossibly thick yellow pages. He glanced up and chuckled. "Don't worry about it. Whatever you put on is going to come off so fast it's going to make your head spin."

Christy chose a soft pink suit she'd purchased the year before at Easter. Carrying it with her into the bathroom, she closed the door. Quite by accident she caught her reflection in the mirror above the sink and gasped at the pitiful sight she made.

Leaning over the sink, she studied the woman who boldly stared back at her. Her short dark hair was a mess, as if it hadn't been combed in weeks. She would be the envy of punk rockers everywhere if she had the courage to step out her front door.

She smiled, and fine lines creased her forehead. Her eyes were another thing. Christy had always considered her distinctive blue eyes to be her best feature. Now they appeared red-rimmed and bloodshot as if she'd been on a two-day drunken spree. Her lips were red and swollen, although she attributed that to Cody's kisses. That man could kiss like no one she'd ever known. She went weak all over again, remembering the feel and taste of his mouth over hers.

Bracing her hands against the sink, she was forced to admit that she was probably the most pathetic creature on the face of the earth. Yet Cody had looked at her as if she were a freshly crowned beauty queen, as if she were gorgeous just the way she was.

The man most definitely loved her. That worked out well since she most definitely loved him.

Cody couldn't keep still. He'd been pacing Christy's living room almost from the moment he'd arrived. He couldn't seem to make himself stop. Four steps, turn, four more steps, turn once again.

He glanced at his watch. She was already five minutes past the hour she'd told him she'd need. What could be taking her so long? She'd locked herself in the bathroom, and he hadn't heard a peep from her since. His mind was beginning to play cruel tricks on him. Perhaps she'd changed her mind about going through with the wedding, and not wanting to hurt his feelings, she'd climbed out the bathroom window and disappeared.

That thought revealed the shocking state of his mental condition more than anything he'd said or done in the past two hours. He'd flown into Seattle with one purpose. Either he'd settle this craziness with Christy or end their relationship.

He hadn't counted on her enthusiasm. She'd been giddy with happiness when he'd first arrived. Okay, he was the giddy one. He hadn't a clue she was going to throw herself into his arms the moment she opened the door. Not that he'd minded; he'd been more than ready to have her in his arms. A slow smile worked at his mouth. Everything had progressed naturally from there.

Cody had always thought of himself as a strong man. Not overly muscular or brawny, although he could hold his own, and often had. His real strength, he felt, was his stubborn determination. He liked to think he had a will of iron.

Christy had proved him wrong in world-record time.

Mentally he'd set the boundaries of how far anything physical should progress between the two of them. Not once had he even considered their lovemaking would advance to such a state.

During the early-morning flight, he'd given himself a pep talk, outlining everything he intended to say to her. He planned to meet with her, explain his position and ask her as calmly and unemotionally as possible to make her decision.

It was either James or him.

If she chose the attorney, without a word of argument, Cody was prepared to accept her choice serenely, and walk out of her life.

Other than the rocky beginning, everything had gone as he'd hoped. Never mind that Christy had managed to break down his resolve within five seconds. The instant she was in his arms, he could feel himself start to weaken.

No woman, not even Becca, had had as much control over him.

Now he and Christy were flying into Coeur d'Alene, Idaho, and getting married. Smiling softly, Cody relaxed against the back of the sofa. He recalled when

Russ and Taylor had arrived back in Cougar Point after serving as chaperons for the drill team. They'd traveled with a busload of high school girls to Reno. The two had left Cougar Point, barely speaking to each other, and arrived back home a few days later married.

Cody could still recall how surprised everyone was. Most folks agreed Taylor was the best thing ever to happen to the opinionated Russ Palmer, but there were several skeptics.

Rightly so. Taylor was a city girl. Russ was a rancher. Taylor had only been in town three months. Doubts that the two could find happiness were as thick as August mosquitoes.

When folks around town learn Cody had married Christy after knowing her less than a month, there were sure to be a fair share of raised eyebrows.

That fact didn't disturb Cody in the least. He loved Christy beyond a doubt, and next month when he stood before the good citizens of Custer County to be sworn in as sheriff, she would be at his side. It would be the proudest moment of his life, and he wanted her with him.

The bathroom door opened, and Christy stepped out. Cody twisted around to inform her she was twelve minutes late. Whatever teasing comment he was about to make wilted before ever making it to his lips.

She was stunningly beautiful, dressed in a pink linen suit. Her hair was perfect, her makeup flawlessly applied. Christy Manning was so beautiful, Cody couldn't help staring at her. It took more effort than he could believe just to close his mouth. He was too tongue-tied to utter a single word.

"Do I look all right?" she asked, gazing up at him expectantly.

For the life of him, all Cody could do was nod.

Christy smiled and held out her gloved hand. "Then let's get this show on the road."

The ceremony itself took place later that same evening in a wedding chapel overlooking the crystal blue waters of Lake Coeur d'Alene. Between the time they obtained the license, purchased a pair of gold bands and made the arrangements for the wedding itself, Cody half expected Christy to voice some doubts.

She didn't. In fact, when it came to repeating their vows, it was Christy's strong, clear voice that stood out in his mind. He couldn't help marveling at how confident and poised she sounded.

The flight back to Seattle brought them into the airport shortly before midnight. In the space of one day Cody had traveled in a jumbo jet from Montana to Washington State, then had flown a two-seater Cessna from Seattle to Coeur d'Alene and back again. He should have been exhausted, but he wasn't. In fact, he was more alive than he could ever remember being in his life. All he had to do was glance at Christy, who delighted in flashing him a sexy, slightly naughty smile, to feel the blood shoot through his veins.

It was with some difficulty that Cody kept the spring out of his step as they returned the Cessna to the hangar and headed toward the rental car. He held open the door for her and pressed a light kiss across her lips when she climbed inside. She sagged against him, and it took every ounce of his restraint not to deepen the kiss.

It took a moment for his mind to clear. "Where to, Mrs. Franklin?" he asked, scooting behind the wheel of the car.

She responded with a blank look.

"Choose any hotel you want." He wanted the best Seattle had to offer for Christy. A honeymoon suite. Champagne. Silk sheets. Room service.

"But I didn't think to pack anything," she protested.

Cody was about to comment that she wasn't going to need any clothes for what he had in mind, but he didn't get the chance.

"I have this white silk baby doll gown. Would you mind terribly much if we went back to my apartment so I could put a few things together?"

"Your wish is my command. I plan to spoil you, Mrs. Franklin."

Pressing her head against his shoulder, Christy sighed audibly and murmured, "I like that trait in a man."

Once at the apartment complex, he went inside with Christy. His own suitcase had remained there.

Christy moved into the bedroom, then reappeared a moment later. She smiled shyly up at him, then flattened her hands on his chest. Cody gazed down at her, meaning to question her, but before he could she slipped her arms around his neck, leaned into him and kissed him soundly.

Cody's response was immediate. He cradled the back of her head, holding her captive as he placed slow, drugging kisses over her soft mouth. Soon she was weak and pliant in his arms.

"What was that for?" he asked when he found his breath.

"Because I'm so happy to be your wife."

Cody was having one hell of a time keeping his hands still. He locked them at the small of her back when it would have been so natural to ease his palms over that sweet, rounded bottom of hers. He glanced longingly toward her bedroom.

Christy reached up, kissed his cheek and deftly removed the Stetson from his head. Cody frowned, wondering at her game, when she tossed it Frisbee fashion across the room. It landed on a chintz-covered cushion as if he'd set it there himself.

Next her fingers were busy working loose the knot of his tie. "Christy?" Her name tumbled from his lips. "What are you doing?"

"Undressing my husband. I've decided I don't want to go to any hotel room, not when we're both here. Not when I can't wait another moment for us to act like an old married couple."

"You're sure?" He didn't know why he was questioning her; he wanted her so much that he was trembling.

"Very sure." Her attention was centered on his front. After discarding his tie and tossing it aside, she started fiddling with his shirt buttons.

Cody's hands roved her back, his fingers seeking and not finding a zipper.

With trembling fingers she peeled open his front and lightly ran the ends of her long nails down his bare chest. Shudders swirled down his spine as she nuzzled his neck, nibbling and sucking and licking her way to the throbbing hollow of his throat and downward over his breastbone.

"Christy," he pleaded, his hands roaming her buttocks. "Where's the damn zipper to your skirt?"

Smiling, she broke away long enough to remove the suit jacket and kick off her heels. Both went flying in opposite directions. She twisted around and unfastened the button at her side, then slid the zipper open enough for the skirt to sigh past her hips and pool at her feet. Stepping out of it, she reached behind her for the row of buttons that ran down the back of her silk blouse.

"I can do that." He sounded as eager as a first-grader offering to hand out papers to his class, Cody realized, but he didn't care. His fingers fumbled awkwardly with the tiny buttons, but he managed. Her blouse and her lacy bra followed the path of his shirt, landing on the carpet somewhere between the sofa and television.

Unable to wait a second longer, Cody kissed her, his tongue surging into her mouth to find hers in a familiar game of sleek caresses. The minute she leaned into him, grazing his bare chest with her full breasts, Cody felt his body heat rise to the boiling point.

Skin to skin. One smooth and velvety, the other as coarse as burlap.

Looping her arms around his neck, Christy let her head fall back. Slowly, sensually, she rotated her puckered nipples over his hard chest.

He groaned, fighting the rising flames of his passion. She was slowly, surely, driving him out of his mind.

"Christy," he begged, not knowing exactly what he was pleading for. Not for her to stop, that much he knew. More, he decided. He needed more of her.

Tucking his arms behind her knees, he lifted her into his arms and carried her into the bedroom. The only light was the soft illumination from the single lamp in a far corner of the living room.

Gently he placed her on the bed, and they hastily finished undressing each other. Cody looked down on her, nestled in the thick folds of a lavender comforter. She was so beautiful that for a moment he was lost to

everything but the woman before him. He longed to tell
her everything he was feeling, and knew it would be
impossible to put into words.

Lightly he ran his hands over her breasts and smiled
at their immediate response. He watched, fascinated, as
her nipples hardened, seeming to pout up at him, seek
his attention and beg for his touch. Bending forward,
he took one needy bobbin in his mouth to wash with his
tongue. For several minutes he staked his claim on her
ripe body.

Christy buckled beneath him and moaned, pleading
for more. A low, growling sound came from deep in his
throat as Cody devoted his mouth to her breasts, sam-
pling, sucking.

Bracing his knees against the side of the mattress, he
kissed her. Their mouths were starved for each other,
and the kisses soon became wild and groping. Christy
folded her arms around his neck and arched her back,
moving against him in ways that staggered his reason.
His mind was whirling, coherent thought beyond him.
Had the roof caved in on top of them, Cody doubted he
would have noticed. They were eager for each other.
Excited and ready.

At least Cody was ready. He had been from the moment Christy had sent his hat sailing across the room.

He shifted his position slightly, his hard length poised
above her, his legs bracketing hers. Unselfishly opening herself to him, Christy made a warm, cozy cradle
for the lower half of his body. Too warm. He pressed
against her, nestling in the patch of dark hair.

With every ounce of self-control Cody possessed, he
tried to hold himself back, but delaying taking her a
second longer was beyond his limits. His mouth met

hers in a frenzy of need, their tongues mating as he slowly sank his body into hers.

Christy's hips came completely off the mattress, rising to meet him. Then she tore her mouth from his and bit down hard on her lower lip.

Cody's eyes flew open. Dear, sweet mother of God, she was a virgin.

In a panic he started to withdraw, but she stopped him.

"No, please, don't stop."

"I'll hurt you more."

"No...it's so good. Oh, Cody, it really is good." On her own she began to thrash about, driving him to the brink of insanity.

She withered mindlessly beneath him, her fingers clenching his shoulders and back in wordless demand. Cody couldn't control himself a second longer, and he thrust deep within her golden warmth.

Christy surged up to meet him, and when his explosion came, Cody was convinced he'd never known pleasure more profound.

Afterward he lay on his back with Christy beside him, her head on his shoulder, her arm draped over his chest. Cody sighed as she cuddled her soft, feminine body intimately against his.

"You should have told me," he whispered, and kissed her brow.

Her eyes remained closed, her smile dreamy. "I told you I was a very good girl."

"I never suspected..."

"Would you have done anything differently?"

Her question gave him pause. His first thought was that he would have been gentler, gone slower. There were any number of ways he could have eased this first time for her had he known. In retrospect, though, Cody wondered if he would have been capable of any of it. By the time he was tightly gloved within her, the walls of his self-control had long since crumbled.

"Oh, Cody..." Christy moaned, and bit into her lower lip.

"I...don't think we should... Not again. There hasn't been enough time for you."

"Don't you dare stop. Not yet." She arched her back and gripped the headboard with both hands, her body pulsing with pleasure.

"Christy... Sweet heaven..."

"What are you doing now?" Cody murmured.

He was half asleep, Christy noted as she caught his earlobe between her teeth. "I'm making a citizen's arrest."

"Oh, yeah! What's the charge?"

"I haven't any yet. I'll trump up some later."

"Christy, hey, what's that? Could it be the sexy silk gown you were telling me about?"

"Never you mind."

"I mind. I like you better with nothing on."

Ignoring his complaints, she straddled his hips and leaned forward, planting her hands on his hair-matted chest, glorying in the control she had over him. "My, my, look what I found."

"What?"

"A dimple. A sexy-as-hell dimple."

"I don't have any damn dimples."

"Oh, but you do. Right here, and here, and here." Her tongue marked each spot until he shivered helplessly.

He recovered quickly. "Hmm, you smell good... flowers, I think."

"Remember, it was you who emptied an entire bottle of bubble bath into my tub."

"You didn't object."

"How could I? You were doing your husbandly duty and washing me... only..." She paused and sucked in a soft breath as he closed his hands over her breasts, kneading the pliant flesh. "I didn't know it could be done in a tub."

"It?" he teased, his nimble tongue branding her nipples before capturing his treasures and sucking lightly.

"Cody, I was supposed to be the one arresting you, remember?"

"Say it." He raised the silk gown high on her leg and began to caress her inner thighs with both hands.

"It embarrasses me to say it... Cody," she whimpered as his finger parted her, executing the sweetest of punishments at the mere hint of her rebellion.

"You are going to say it."

She couldn't utter a single word. Rivers of molten fire spread through her. She didn't know her body was capable of giving her any more pleasure than it already had. Then Cody burrowed deeper into the moist folds of her womanhood, and Christy found her hips grinding in blind submission.

"I love it when you blush."

Christy sighed and closed her eyes, her head resting on the hard planes of his chest, her hand pressed over his heart. The steady, even thud of his pulse was slowly lulling her to sleep. "Are we ever going to rest?"

"Nope. The way I figure it we've got a little less than forty-eight hours before my plane leaves, and at the rate we're going we can make love—"

"I'm too tired."

Christy felt his smile against the crown of her head. "I am too... We'll make up for lost time in the morning."

"In the morning," she echoed as her eyes slowly drifted closed.

A horrible racket woke Christy from a deep sleep several hours later. It sounded as if an explosion had taken place inside her apartment. She bolted upright and glanced at her clock radio.

Cody was already out of bed and was reaching for his pants.

"Christy?"

The slurred voice belonged to none other than her brother Rich. She'd given him an extra key to her apartment. He stopped in often, but had always phoned first.

"It's my brother. He has a key. Stay here. I'll get rid of him."

"Your brother?"

"Shh." She reached for her robe, then kissed Cody before moving into the living room.

Rich stood just inside the door, looking very much like an errant schoolboy. "Hi," he said, raising his right hand.

"I don't suppose you know what time of the night it is?"

"Late," he offered.

"How about early."

"How early?"

"Too early," she told him, praying he wouldn't notice the two sets of clothes spread from one end of the living room to the other. She marched across the room and gripped his elbow, directing him toward the front door.

He gave her a hurt look. "You're sending me back into the cold?"

"Yes."

"I didn't drive here. I couldn't, not in my condition," he argued. "I know you probably can't tell, but I've had a teeny bit too much to drink."

"I noticed."

"I was hoping you'd fill me with black coffee, listen to my woes and let me sleep on your couch."

"I have to be at work in two hours." A slight exaggeration. When she didn't show up at the office, everyone would assume she was still home sick with the flu.

"Pamela did me wrong," Rich blurted out. "I need some advice and I need it from a woman. Just hear me out, okay?"

Not knowing what else she could do, Christy moved into her kitchen and started assembling a pot of coffee. Rich pulled out a stool at her kitchen counter and plopped himself down. "Apparently she's been seeing him all along."

"Who?"

"Pamela."

"No, who's she been seeing?" This conversation was quickly frustrating Christy.

"Hell if I know his name. Some jerk."

"It isn't like you were crazy about her."

"Maybe not, but I always thought she was crazy about me. What is it with women these days? Isn't anyone faithful anymore?"

"Ah..."

Rich squinted into the darkened living room. "Hey, what's going on here?" Standing, he walked over to the chintz-covered chair and picked up Cody's Stetson. He glanced back at his sister and frowned.

"I can explain," she offered weakly.

Frowning, he walked into the kitchen and carefully placed the Stetson on her head. Several sizes too large, it rested well below her hairline in the middle of her forehead.

"Is there something you wanted to tell me?" he asked.

Chapter Twelve

"Who the hell are you?" Rich demanded.

Christy shoved the Stetson farther back on her head to find Cody walking out of the bedroom.

"It sounded like you might need a little help explaining matters," her husband said casually.

Rich pointed his finger at his sister while his mouth made troutlike movements. His gaze had narrowed, and disdain and disbelief marked his handsome features. Like his brothers, Rich was tall, dark-haired and possessed the same incredible blue eyes.

"It's not as bad as it looks," Christy said, ignoring his censure. Nonchalantly she poured him a cup of coffee.

Swiveling his gaze between Cody and Christy, Rich shook his head. "It looks pretty damn bad, little sister." His gaze followed the trail of clothing scattered across the beige living room carpet. His mouth twisted with disgust as he started toward the front door. "In fact, I don't think I've got the stomach to listen to you."

"You'll hear her out," Cody warned grimly, walking toward Rich. The two men stood no more than two feet apart, glaring at each other like prizefighters waiting to trade blows. The air crackled with electricity.

"And who's going to make me listen? You?" Rich's sarcasm was sharp and bitter. "If that's what you think, then I've got news for you, cowboy."

"Rich, kindly shut your mouth," Christy pleaded. "The least you can do is hear me out."

"I don't listen to—"

"Don't say it," Cody interrupted, his words so cold they froze in midair. "Because if you do, you'll live to regret it."

Rich mocked him with a smile. "Listen, Mr. Marlboro Man, I've taken about enough from you—"

"Stop it, both of you," Christy cried, marching out from her kitchen. She stood between her husband and her brother, a hand on each man's chest, feeling as though she were braced between two giant pillars. She glanced up at Rich. "I'd like to introduce you to my husband, Cody Franklin. Cody, this stupid oaf is my third youngest brother, Rich."

"Your husband!"

"My husband," she echoed softly. She dropped her hands and slipped her arm around Cody's waist, leaning against him, needing his solid strength.

"I'll have you know," Cody muttered, "you interrupted my wedding night."

"Your husband," Rich repeated a second time, striding across the room. He retrieved Christy's bra from the floor, picked it up with one finger and twirled it around a couple of times. "I don't suppose James knows about this?"

Christy snatched her underwear out of her brother's hands. "As a matter of fact, he doesn't."

"This is getting all the more interesting." Sitting on the sofa, he retrieved Cody's shirt and made a soft tsking sound with his tongue. "What about Mom and Dad?"

"They don't know, either," Cody said forcefully.

"Aha," Rich snickered, "the plot thickens."

"I'm so pleased you find this amusing." Christy hastily moved about the room, picking up several pieces of discarded clothing, more embarrassed than she could ever remember being.

Cody poured himself a cup of coffee and joined Rich, sitting on the opposite end of the sofa. "I'm a good friend of Russ Palmer's," he said by way of explanation.

Rich nodded. "So my dear, sweet sister met you when she was in Montana visiting Taylor?"

"Cody's the one who drove her to the hospital," Christy added. She sat on the side of the sofa and curved her arm around Cody's broad shoulders.

"Then this was something of a whirlwind courtship." Rich paused and studied the two of them. "Exactly how long have you known each other?"

"Long enough," Cody answered, making it plain he didn't much care for this line of questioning.

"We didn't mean to fall in love so fast," Christy continued, wanting to untangle any doubts Rich had about her relationship with Cody. "It just happened."

"You might have mentioned it to James."

"I probably should have phoned and told him while I was still in Montana, but it seemed so discourteous to break the engagement over the phone, and then when I arrived home—''

"The surprise engagement party," Rich said, groaning loudly. "You were trapped. Mom put her heart and soul into that silly party. You couldn't back out without humiliating her. Not at the last minute like that."

"I wanted to tell James right away, but that didn't work out, either." The hopelessness of the entire situation nearly overwhelmed her. "The Mulligan trial was called early, and he's immersed himself in what is sure to be the most complicated case of his career. He's got to be emotionally and physically at his peak for that."

"Hell, that's right," Rich commented. "I'd forgotten about that."

"The timing couldn't be worse for me to tell James about Cody and me."

Rich released a long, sympathetic sigh. "You do seem to have your problems, little sister."

Cody leaned against the back of the sofa. "You can imagine how I felt when I learned she'd been roped into attending the engagement party. To complicate matters, she set a date for the wedding."

Rich did a pitiful job of disguising a smile. "November 12, wasn't it?"

"You're not being cute, Rich, so cut the comedy, will you?" Christy playfully punched his upper arm.

"You have to admit, it's more than a little amusing."

Christy found damn little of their situation entertaining. She was deliriously pleased to be Cody's wife, but he was flying out of Seattle in another day, and she'd be forced into returning to her job and living a farce. She wouldn't be able to keep up this charade long without losing her sanity.

"Perhaps this predicament is comical to someone else," Cody confessed grudgingly, "but trust me, it isn't if you're one of the parties involved."

Rich was quick to agree with a short shake of his head. "So the two of you decided to take matters into your own hands and get married."

Christy nodded. Her eyes happened to meet Cody's, and they exchanged a loving, promising look. His fingers linked with her. "It must sound crazy."

"Hey, it works for me," Rich said, clearly having trouble keeping the delight out of his voice. "But personally I wouldn't be in your shoes for all the tea in China when you tell Mom and Dad what you did."

"Why not?" Cody asked with a dark frown.

"They were cheated out of one wedding when Taylor married Russ without a single family member present. I can only speculate what they'll say when they hear Christy did the same thing."

"They'll skin me alive," she muttered. In all the excitement, in all her enthusiasm, Christy had forgotten how much her mother was looking forward to planning her wedding. Her plans were far more elaborate than the engagement party. On the way out of the Eagles Hall that dreadful night, Elizabeth Manning had been filled with ideas and opinions and excitement.

"Your parents won't do any such thing," Cody insisted without the least bit of reservation.

"Cody, you don't know them." Christy felt close to tears. Elizabeth Manning might never forgive her, and she'd always done what her mother thought best. Until now.

"They won't say a word," he insisted softly, "because I won't let them."

"But you don't understand . . ."

"If your parents are looking for someone to blame, they can deal with me. I was the one who insisted we marry now. You went along with it."

"Because I'm crazy in love with you and because I wanted to be your wife more than I've ever wanted anything."

"Hey," Rich said, gesturing with both hands, "if both of you want to stand in front of the firing squad, I'm not going to stop you."

A chill descended over the room like an arctic wind. "I take it there was a reason for this unexpected visit," Cody said pointedly.

"I was having woman problems," Rich mumbled, frowning.

"I thought there must have been something troubling you the night of the party." Although Rich wasn't enlightening her with the details, Christy should have known something was amiss. Otherwise he would have noticed how distressed the entire evening was making her.

"I may be having a few problems," Rich continued. "But trust me, they're nothing compared to what the two of you are facing. Married to one man while engaged to another—that, little sister, takes the cake."

"How kind of you to point it out." Yawning, she covered her mouth with the back of her hand. "I'll make you up a bed on the sofa and you can spend the rest of the night there."

"And interrupt your honeymoon?"

"It's already been interrupted," Cody grimly reminded the other man. "If there's the least bit of justice in this world, I'll be able to return the favor someday."

"No chance of that happening. I'm swearing off women. The whole lot of them," Rich warned with an emphatic shake of his head.

"Oh?" Christy had heard that song before.

"It's true. They're fickle, money-hungry bloodsuckers."

"Thank you very much," Christy said, standing.

"With a few possible exceptions." He eyed his sister and smiled momentarily in rapid apology. "Damn few."

"Now where was it you said you wanted to go for dinner?" Cody asked, reaching for his suit jacket.

"What's the matter with eating here?" Christy asked, not wanting to leave their protected cocoon. Everything had been idyllic, and she was almost light-headed with happiness. To walk outside these protected walls may well invite trouble, and she'd had enough of that to last her a lifetime.

"I thought you wanted to dine out?"

"Not really." At the time he'd made the suggestion, Christy hadn't been able to think of an excuse. Now her mind flooded with them, only she doubted that Cody would consider them sensible.

She checked her freezer and extracted a package of pork chops. "I could wrestle us up some grub in no time." She turned around and grinned. "Am I beginning to sound like a Montana woman?"

"No. You're beginning to sound like a cattle thief." He moved behind her, slipped his arms around her middle and nuzzled the softly scented curve of her neck.

"I'm a good cook."

"I know."

"How could you? Every time I go to make something for us, you interrupt me with . . . you know."

"Are you still having trouble saying the words?"

"No . . ." She giggled softly. "You've cured me of that." Twisting around, she leaned against the refrigerator door with her hands primly linked in front of her. "I can say lovemaking just about as often as you like to do it."

"Then let's get out of here before you give me any ideas."

"I like giving you ideas."

Cody glanced at his watch. "It's well past the dinner hour and I'm hungry."

She moistened her lips with the tip of her tongue. "You want me to whisper some of the other words you've taught me?"

"Christy . . . no."

"Come here." She beckoned him with her index finger. "I'll whisper a couple of humdingers in your ear."

Cody ignored her summons. "I'm not going to let you sidetrack me."

"Oh, but I enjoy sidetracking you so much."

"That's the problem," Cody said. "I like it just as much." He cleared his throat and changing tactics, reached for his hat and said, "As your husband, I command that we leave for dinner now."

"You command?" She couldn't help smiling, although she was trying hard not to.

"That's right," he said firmly. "I've got to teach you early on in this marriage that I'm the one wearing the pants in this family."

"If that's the case, then why are they so often unzipped?"

Cody actually blushed, and Christy smiled widely.

"Because I'm a needy husband," he countered gruffly. "Are you complaining?"

"No." She tossed him a saucy grin. "I happen to be a needy wife. In fact, I seem to be experiencing a need right now. Is it hot in here to you?"

"Christy?" Cody's voice contained a low note of warning.

"It seems terribly hot...much too hot for all these clothes." She jerked the light sweater over her head and let it fall to the floor. Next she lowered the straps of her bra, pushing them down far enough to expose the tops of her breasts. "There," she said with a deep, husky sigh that gently raised and lowered her shoulders, offering Cody what she hoped was a tantalizing display of her assets. "That feels worlds better."

Cody stood his ground for a couple of minutes more. His Adam's apple bobbed in his throat once before he removed his hat and sent it flying across the room.

Silently Christy rejoiced. She was only now beginning to grasp the power she wielded over her husband.

"What about those jeans? Aren't they making you hot, too?" Cody asked.

"Maybe they are at that. Only I can't seem to work open the snap." He didn't seem to notice she hadn't tried.

"I see." He stepped over to her, holding himself stiff. His jaw was clenched hard, his mouth a tight line. He made short work of her bra, then cupped Christy's breasts, his hands firm and insistent.

Sighing, Christy closed her eyes, giving herself over to a host of warm sensations. Cody employed one hand, stroking her breast, tracing her nipple with his thumb until it ached. His other hand was busy at the opening of her jeans. The zipper purred, and Christy was filled with another small sense of triumph.

She shivered helplessly as Cody slid the thick material of her jeans down the soft, womanly curve of her hips. Her bikini underwear followed until both rested at her feet.

One hand administered unbridled attention to her breast while the other stroked the silky smoothness at the inside of her thigh. The back of her head was pressed against the refrigerator door, her eyes closed. Anticipation caused her breath to come in choppy interludes.

Cody kissed her with a savage hunger, his mouth shaping hers, consuming her. "Open your legs to me," he whispered between greedy kisses.

Christy complied willingly and whimpered softly as his fingers deftly parted her. A sweet, building tenderness swept through her until she was dizzy with the magnitude of her love for him. Never had she dreamed loving a man could be so keenly pleasurable.

"Is this what you want?" He teased her womanhood with a slow series of delicious forays, tormented her with long, delicate strokes calculated to drive her toward the breathless climb of release.

"Yes . . . yes."

His fingers went still. "Do you want more?"

"Yes . . ." Of their own accord her hips started to grind, seeking the sweet oblivion of deliverance. "Cody . . . don't stop." Her hands were anchored in his hair, her hips thrashing, demanding what he suddenly didn't seem willing to give her.

"I'm your husband."

"Yes..." Why he chose now to remind her of the fact was something of a mystery, but not one Christy cared to mull over.

"You're my wife?"

"Yes," she groaned softly, and bit hard into her lower lip as he continued to plunder her. He spread feather-light kisses over her breasts until each nipple quivered and throbbed.

"Then you'll do as I wish?" As if to induce her into an appropriate response, he suckled at one pebbled nipple until her hips buckled. The hot sensation that shot through her was indescribable. Incredible.

"Anything..." Her nails bit into his shoulders as he slowly, willfully, explored the innermost part of her body. Christy tossed back her head as she climbed higher and higher, prepared to beg for the magic he offered.

"Dinner... out?" he asked next.

The fiery pleasure washed over her. "Oh, yes, anywhere you want... just don't stop."

"Don't worry, love. I have no intention of doing that for a good long time."

Christy's gaze fell reluctantly on Cody's luggage, which was spread open across the top of her mattress. The lump in her throat was growing tighter by the minute. She'd decided earlier that she wasn't going to be emotional when he left. They'd talked everything out earlier, planned for their future as best they could.

"You called the office?" Cody asked, tucking a clean shirt into the suitcase.

"Yes... I told them I still had the flu." Lying didn't come easy to Christy. She felt as though she'd dug herself into a deep pit.

"What did they say?"

"Marcia, she's the office manager, claimed it was a slow week and not to worry about it, but she did make a point of asking me if I'd be in on Friday, which seemed a little odd."

"James?"

"He was at the courthouse." Her eyes rounded at the unexpectedness of the question.

"When was the last time you heard from him?"

"Ah..." She had to stop and think about it. "The day following the engagement party. We talked briefly, and he explained that he wouldn't have much time to keep in touch while the trial was going on." Under normal circumstances she would have seen him at the office even if it was for a few minutes every morning. The fact that he hadn't made an effort to contact her said a good deal about their relationship, or rather their lack of one.

"I see." Cody was noticeably surprised.

"He's very intense and single-minded."

"Do you think he'll get an acquittal?"

"I don't know," she said, sighing softly.

"Whatever happens, this can't go on much longer. You realize that, don't you?"

"It won't be more than a few days," she promised. In discussing the situation they'd agreed on a time limit. Even if the trial dragged on for more than a week, Christy had promised to return James's diamond ring and tell her parents that she and Cody were married.

"I still think it would be best if we told your parents now."

"Not yet," she pleaded, needing time. The way Christy figured it, she would start dropping hints so the fact she'd married Cody wouldn't come as a big sur-

prise. After Cody flew back to Montana, she intended
to stop over at the family home and casually point out
that James hadn't contacted her once since the engagement party. She was hoping her parents would con-
clude that perhaps James wouldn't be the best husband
for her, after all.

"Christy, I'm worried." Her husband stood in front
of her, cupping her shoulders. His eyes were darker than
normal, his face tight with concern. "I don't like leaving you, and the circumstances make it all the more
difficult."

"You know I love you."

His mouth curved into a slow, sensual smile. "Beyond a doubt."

"Good." She slipped her arms around his waist and
hugged him close. Her ear was pressed over his heart,
which beat strongly and evenly, offering her reassur-
ance. In time they'd be able to look back on these bleak
days and laugh. Someday, but not now.

"I'll phone you twice a day," he promised in a husky
whisper. "Morning and night."

"I'll need that."

"So will I."

A sigh of regret rumbled through his chest as he
dropped his arms. "It's time to go."

Neither of them seemed inclined to talk on the ride to
the airport. When it came time for Cody to board the
Boeing 737, he hugged Christy close and kissed her
lightly. It was as if he dared not kiss her the way they
both enjoyed for fear he wouldn't be able to walk away
from her. She understood all too well.

She smoothed her hand over his shoulder, needing to
touch him because letting him board the plane was so

damn difficult. Her eyes managed to avoid his. "Take care of yourself."

"You, too."

She nodded, barely conscious of the way she clung to him. "Of course. It shouldn't be more than a few days. Before we know it we'll be together."

"And next time we won't need to think about parting." His words were heavy and grim.

His flight was announced one last time, and Cody darted a look over his shoulder toward the jetway and the flight attendant who was waiting to take the ticket. "I've got to go."

She closed her eyes tightly in an effort to keep from weeping, and nodded.

Cody kissed her again, only this time his mouth was fierce and wild as if he felt the need to punish her, punish them both. He released her by degrees, his reluctance tearing at her heart. With everything that was in her, Christy longed to board the plane with him. How much easier it would be to leave with Cody and then write James and her parents. But Christy knew she couldn't walk away from her responsibilities and live with herself. Cody understood that, too, she was certain of it. Christy Manning Franklin had always done the right thing, sometimes for the wrong reasons.

When the plane rolled down the runway, Christy was there to see the jet take off and slice through the thick white clouds. Her heart felt as if it were ready to burst, when in actuality she had much to be grateful for. She was married to the man she loved and would be joining him soon.

The following morning Christy returned to work for the first time since she'd left for her vacation. What a difference a few weeks could make. She wasn't even the same woman as the one who had left.

"Christy." James's voice was elevated as he stepped over to her desk. "You're back. I hope you're feeling better."

For all his brilliance, a good deal of life had escaped James Wilkens. He smiled and reached for her hand, lightly squeezing her fingers. Kissing her, even in an empty office, would have been unthinkable. He'd never been openly affectionate, but he was tender and good, and Christy couldn't dismiss her guilty conscience.

"I'm much better, thanks. How's the Mulligan case going?"

He frowned and briefly looked away before responding. "Not good."

"How much longer do you think it's going to take?"

"I'm hoping to wrap everything up by the end of next week."

"That long?" She couldn't keep the disappointment out of her voice.

James frowned anew. "I didn't realize how negatively this case was affecting you."

"It's just that..." She couldn't very well announce she was looking for the right moment to tell him she was married to someone else.

"I know, darling." He said the last word softly, as though fearing someone might overhear him speaking tenderly to her. Knowing James as well as she did, Christy knew this was completely daring on his part. "This is a difficult time for us both, but it will be over soon, and then we can both get on with our lives."

Now that Christy had time to study the attorney, he seemed more peaked than usual. Deep lines were etched around his eyes and mouth. It was apparent James wasn't sleeping well.

"The case is going far more poorly than you'd like me to believe, isn't it?"

James sighed. "It's difficult to hide these things from the one you love. Yes, much worse than I'd anticipated."

"Is there anything I can do?" Christy found herself asking. James was the type of man who would remain calm and cool in an earthquake. Nothing panicked him, little disrupted him. If it weren't for the fact that she was well acquainted with him, Christy would never have guessed he was experiencing troubles with this case.

"Nothing," he said, and granted her a rare smile. "But your concern is greatly appreciated." He checked his watch. "It's time I left for the courthouse. I won't be back for the rest of the day."

Christy nodded.

"I suppose we should meet for dinner. After all, it's been a long time since we've gone out. But—"

"Don't worry," Christy interrupted. "I understand." If she was having trouble dealing with a short conversation on his way out the door, an entire evening in each other's company would have been unbearable.

"Have a good day," he said gently.

"You, too."

He nodded, but his expression was somber. It was all too apparent that he didn't anticipate having anything resembling a satisfactory day.

At lunchtime Christy looked up to find Marcia standing at her desk. The office manager had been with the firm over fifteen years and was one of the finest women Christy knew.

Christy smiled. "Do you need something?" After a three-week absence, her desk was piled high with folders.

"Can you come into one of the conference rooms for a minute?"

"Sure." Christy hadn't a clue what was going on. Marcia looked exceptionally pleased about something, which led Christy to believe that whatever it was had little if anything to do with the amount of work she'd missed.

Leading the way, her friend paused in front of the wide oak doors and grinned sheepishly. "It's good to have you back, Christy. It made all of us appreciate how much your bright smile adds to our day." With that she opened the door.

Christy was greeted with a chorus of "Surprise" from her fellow workers. A large cake rested in the center of the table, surrounded by several gaily wrapped packages. She must have looked stunned, because Marcia placed her hand around her shoulder, smiled and explained. "It's a wedding shower for you and James."

Chapter Thirteen

A week had passed since Cody had left. By far the longest week of his life. He wanted Christy with him, hungered for the sight of her smile and the way her eyes darkened when she looked up at him in that suggestive way that spelled out her desire.

Almost from the first time they'd met, Cody had known he loved Christy. Marrying her had helped him deal with the ridiculous set of circumstances in which they found themselves trapped.

He still wasn't pleased that she remained engaged to James, but there seemed little he could say or do about it. If it had been up to him, he'd have settled it before flying out of Seattle, but Christy had been adamant she was doing the right thing by waiting. Cody wasn't nearly as convinced, but the decision had been hers, and he didn't feel he could go against Christy's wishes.

So they were man and wife. Cody felt married. It was as if he'd lived his entire life waiting for this woman. In the too-brief days they'd been together, Cody had changed. The difference in him wasn't something detectable to the naked eye. His life's purpose had always been focused on his career, and in many ways it still was. Christy, however, added a new dimension to his personality.

She'd taught him to dream.

Unlike Russ, who'd always anticipated marriage, Cody had given up hope of ever finding the right woman. It hadn't been a conscious decision. In fact, he hadn't been fully aware of it until he'd met Christy. He was deeply involved and committed to law enforcement. The fact he'd married wouldn't change that, but it gave his life a deeper meaning.

Hell, he mused, he was getting downright philosophical. Christy had exposed new facets of his personality he didn't even know existed.

Anyone brighter would have guessed what was happening the first time they'd kissed. He still recalled feeling lost and bewildered. When he learned she was engaged to marry James, Cody had been shaken more than he dared to admit even to himself.

James. The other man's name brought a grim frown to Cody's forehead. Reluctantly Christy had shown him a picture of the attorney. He looked clean-cut, professional and intelligent. Sterile. James Wilkens lacked, Cody guessed from that brief analysis, passion. It was difficult to imagine James allowing a little thing like falling in love to overcome his inhibitions.

In that sense Cody had been more than fortunate. Had Christy been engaged to any other man, she most certainly wouldn't have been a virgin.

Christy a virgin. That fact had taken him by complete surprise.

He wished he'd known. No, he admitted honestly, he was pleased he hadn't. She'd managed to keep it a secret from him for her own purposes. The woman was incredible. The memory of the way she'd unselfishly offered herself, come to life in his arms, satisfied his every need, made Cody weak.

In an effort to clear his thoughts, he stood, moved into his compact kitchen and poured himself a cup of coffee. He was supposed to be packing, getting ready for his move into Miles City, but because of everything that had transgressed between him and Christy, he'd delayed until the last minute.

Almost everything in the living room was inside cardboard boxes, and absently Cody headed toward the bedroom, intent on getting as much accomplished that evening as he could.

He recognized his mistake almost immediately.

Christy had never slept on his bed, never even been in this room, but the fires she sparked to life within Cody were more evident there than in any other room.

Feeling helpless from missing her so much, Cody sat on the end of the mattress. He'd married himself one little hellcat. A smile tempted his mouth. She was also an angel. How one woman could play two distinct roles so skillfully was beyond Cody.

Christy was an innocent, and yet she'd tutored him in the art of making love. She was a shameless hussy one moment and a guileless virgin the next. She seduced him with her gentle ways, humbled him with his insatiable need for her.

Half the time they were so impatient for each other that they hadn't bothered to use any form of birth control. Briefly they'd discussed that. If she were to get pregnant, Cody wouldn't mind. In many ways it would please him tremendously, although he was willing to admit the timing would be all wrong for her. Christy had enough pressures on her without adding any new ones.

A week. They'd been apart for seven days, and it felt like an eternity. Damn it all, he wanted her with him.

Now. Not two days from now.

Not next week. Now.

His patience was wearing paper-thin. He gave himself several minutes to clear his head before reaching for the phone. Christy answered on the second ring.

Her voice softened when she heard his voice. "Soon," she promised in a sweet, seductive whisper that nearly drove him crazy.

"How soon?" he demanded, doing his best to disguise his growing lack of tolerance.

"A couple more days."

"Forgive me for saying this, but didn't you claim it would be 'a couple of days' a couple of days ago?" His voice was sharp and tight despite his best efforts.

"Yes, but there are complications."

"Aren't there always?"

"Cody, please, don't be angry with me..."

"I called because I love you."

"I love you, too," she confessed, sounding bewildered, and Cody realized he'd probably pushed too hard and quickly backed off, spending the next few minutes telling her of his love.

When he replaced the receiver several minutes later, he was more frustrated than ever.

Cody was enjoying breakfast in the bowling alley early the following morning when Russ showed up. It wasn't unusual for Russ to eat in town, but rarer these days since he'd married Taylor.

The rancher slid into the booth across from Cody. "I thought I'd find you here."

"You looking for me?" he grumbled. The way he was missing Christy, needing Christy, made him a prime candidate for a Dale Carnegie course.

"You could say that." Russ turned over the ceramic mug and waited until the waitress strolled past and filled it for him. He reached for the menu. "You look like hell."

"Nice of you to notice," Cody muttered.

"I didn't come here to pick a fight."

Their friendship was too good for this. "I haven't been sleeping well," Cody admitted reluctantly, sipping from his own coffee in an effort to avoid an interrogation from his best friend. If the truth be known, he hadn't had a decent night's sleep since he'd flown out of Seattle.

"How's Christy holding up?"

"A hell of a lot better than I am." Cody thought she always sounded downright cheerful, as if it were perfectly normal for a couple to be married three days and then separated for weeks on end.

"You sure about that?"

Russ's question caught Cody off guard. He narrowed his gaze as he studied the rancher, wondering if Russ knew something he didn't. Russ's attention seemed captured by the menu.

"I'm not sure of anything," Cody answered thoughtfully. "What makes you ask?"

Typically Russ shrugged. "Nothing in particular." He set aside the menu, declined to order breakfast when

Mary delivered Cody's and sat there looking superior. "Go ahead and eat," he prompted, motioning toward the plate of sliced ham, eggs, hash browns and toast.

"I wasn't planning on letting my meal get cold," Cody informed him frostily. His nerves were shot, and the last thing he needed was his best friend dropping innuendoes at his feet like hand grenades.

Cupping the mug with both hands, Russ leaned back in the booth and stretched his long legs out in front of him. "Who exactly knows you and Christy are married?" he asked after a moment.

"Everyone but James and her parents." Christy's three older brothers were all aware of the fact they'd run off and married. Cody had briefly spoken to the two oldest brothers, Paul and Jason, before he'd left Seattle. Rich had been the first to discover their secret, and he'd quickly let the others in on it.

"Should I thank you that Mrs. Simmons stopped me in the street yesterday with a jar of her watermelon pickles?" Cody asked, eyeing Russ. "She claimed she heard the sheriff had taken himself a wife and wanted to give me a small gift."

"Ah...I might have mentioned something to Mrs. Simmons," Russ said, hiding a smile. Mrs. Simmons handed out homemade preserves at every opportunity. Each family in town ended up with one jar or another of her goodies each year.

"What makes you ask?"

"Nothing in particular," Russ said enigmatically. He took another drink of his coffee. "I guess you and everyone else in town figured out Taylor got pregnant on our honeymoon."

Cody was having trouble following this conversation. "What's that got to do with anything?"

"Nothing," he said, downright cheerfully.

"Listen, Russ, if you know something I don't, just spit it out, would you? I'm in no mood for games. Is something going on with Christy that I don't know about?"

"Did she tell you about the wedding shower?"

Now it was Cody's turn to scowl. "No. When did this happen?"

"Last week. The girls in the office held it for her, threw it as a surprise."

"That was nice."

"It wasn't for you and Christy," Russ barked. "What's with you, man? The shower was for Christy and James."

"Oh, God." Cody rubbed his hand down his face. She hadn't said a word, not a single word about any wedding shower. And now that Russ had said something, maybe, just maybe, Christy did sound a little less like Mary Sunshine than usual. He was fast losing his perspective.

"I bet you she hasn't told you something else, either."

Cody resented like hell having his brother-in-law tell him things Christy wasn't. "You mean there's more?" he asked darkly. "Did her mother decide to take her shopping and spring for a three-thousand-dollar wedding dress?"

"Nothing quite so drastic," Russ said with a hint of a smile. "I overheard Taylor on the phone last night. She was talking to Christy."

"What did Christy say?"

"I don't know. I only heard half of the conversation."

Cody had talked to Christy himself. He'd hung up with a restless feeling he couldn't name, but had attributed it to the fact she was still in Seattle when he wanted her in Montana with him. He was doing his damnedest to be as levelheaded about all this as he could.

"And?"

"And when I questioned Taylor, she seemed reluctant to say much. But I heard her discuss symptoms."

"Symptoms?"

"I tried to tell you earlier," Russ informed him with a look that doubted Cody's intelligence, "but you got so damn defensive, I shut up," Russ remarked testily. "Taylor got pregnant in Reno. Think about it, Cody. Taylor and Christy are two of *five* children. Doesn't it seem obvious to you that the Manning women are a fertile lot?"

"Christy's not pregnant," Cody said with a confidence he wasn't feeling. He felt his head start to spin with the possibility.

"You're sure of that, are you?"

"She would say something if she even suspected. I'd bet on it."

"Of course. She tells you everything."

"I'd like to think she'd confide in me," Cody said, growing more uncertain by the moment.

"If she didn't tell you about the wedding shower, you can damn well wager she wouldn't mention she's hanging her head over a toilet seat every morning."

Cody felt as if he'd been kicked in the stomach. Christy was pregnant and too concerned about protecting her parents and James to risk telling him.

Hell, she couldn't tell him. It all made a weird kind of sense now. How could she share her concerns?

Missing her the way he did, Cody was irritable and impatient while Christy carried the brunt of the load.

Hastily Cody slid out of the booth. He reached for his hat. He'd been looking for an excuse to put an end to this nonsense, and by God, he had one.

"Where you going?" Russ demanded, reaching across the table for Cody's untouched breakfast plate. He leaned forward and retrieved the salt and pepper shakers.

"Seattle."

Chuckling, Russ nodded. "That's what I thought."

"Enjoy your breakfast," Cody muttered sarcastically.

"Thanks," he responded between bites, "I will."

Christy had been feeling blue all day. Cody wasn't home when she'd tried to phone, and that depressed her all the more. Nothing made sense. Nothing. She felt weepy and excited. Confused and elated. Engaged to one man. Married to another. She might be pregnant. It might be the beginning of an ulcer. She didn't know which.

She couldn't sleep, although she desperately needed to.

Her appetite was nil. After going through the hassle of fixing herself spaghetti and a salad for dinner, her dinner sat untouched on her kitchen table.

Feeling wretched, she plopped herself down in front of the television and turned on the movie channel, silently chastising herself for not writing thank-you notes to her friends from the office. Sending notes of appreciation for gifts she fully intended to return seemed a nonsensical thing to do.

A 1940s war movie with an incredibly young John Wayne and Maureen O'Hara was playing, and she was soon caught up in the fast-paced action. How minor her troubles seemed compared to those on the screen.

Damp tissues crowded her end table. She was sniffling ingloriously when her doorbell chimed.

Whoever was on the other side was certainly impatient. The doorbell rang testily a second time before she was halfway across the carpet. "Hold your horses," she said, peevish and disgruntled. She wasn't interested in company.

Christy quickly changed her mind.

"Cody," she whispered when she saw it was her husband. "Oh, Cody." Without another word she broke into tears and flew into his arms.

His mouth was on hers then in that urgent, hungry way that was so familiar between them. Cody directed her back into the living room, then closed the door with his foot, all the while kissing her.

Christy's hands roamed his face when he released her. She giggled and locked her arms around his neck, holding on to him for everything she was worth, and at the moment she felt like the richest lady in town.

"Oh... Christy, I missed you," he breathed, and briefly closed his eyes. His hands caressed the sides of her face, brushing the hair from her brow. He studied her, kissing her again and again as if he'd never get enough of the taste of her.

"I've been so miserable without you," Christy admitted softly, feeling weepy and jubilant at the same time.

"Me, too, love." He kissed her again and again until her lips felt swollen. He looked at her for a long moment, frowning, then smiling, then frowning again.

"What is it?" Christy asked, reading the confusion she saw in him but not understanding it. She found a wonder in him, too, as if he couldn't quite believe even yet that they were married.

Christy believed it. Their love was the only thing that had gotten her through the trauma of the past week.

"Are you pregnant?" he demanded without preamble, running his splayed fingers through her hair. His hold on her tightened slightly, but Christy doubted that Cody was aware of it.

Involuntarily her eyes widened at the unexpectedness of his question. "I...I don't know yet."

"You've been ill?"

"Yes... How'd you know that?" Usually she'd been sick in the morning, but often in the afternoons, too. If she was looking for a pattern, there wasn't one. She was confused and anxious, and not knowing where to turn, she'd contacted her sister. "Taylor?" Christy never dreamed that her older sister would say anything to Cody. She'd counted on Taylor to be discreet.

"No," Cody admitted, scowling. "I had breakfast with Russ this morning. Rather Russ ate *my* breakfast while he cheerfully pointed out that Taylor got pregnant while they were still in Reno and the fact Manning women don't seem to have a problem conceiving."

"You came because of that?"

"No." Cody dropped his hands and stepped away from her. He took a moment to compose his thoughts, and was apparently having some trouble because he anxiously plowed his fingers through his hair. "That's a fair enough question," he went on. "I did come in part because I was afraid...no, afraid's the wrong word. I was concerned for you. I came for another reason, too."

He was so sincere, so forthright. "Yes?"

His eyes darkened. "You didn't tell me about the wedding shower."

Christy dropped her gaze. "I couldn't."

"I realize that now, and I realize a whole lot more. This is the end of it, Christy." His eyes, dark as indigo, burned into hers. "As your husband, I can't and won't allow you to continue this charade any longer."

Spontaneous tears filled her eyes as she nodded. "I don't think I can pull it off another day. I . . . thought I was doing what was best for everyone involved, but I see now I was only prolonging the agony—mostly my own. You were right, so right, there'll never be a good time to tell Mom and Dad. I did us both a terrible disservice by refusing to realize that."

Cody's lips brushed her forehead. "Don't be so hard on yourself."

"There isn't anyone else to blame. It's just that it's so difficult for me to disappoint my parents. I love them both so much, and they're so fond of James."

"But they don't have the right to pick your husband for you."

"I know." She paused and exhaled softly. "I would have liked to have spared James this, but he has to know. I . . . I did him a disfavor by not telling him the first afternoon I arrived home. James isn't the emotionally fragile creature I've made him out to be."

Cody's eyes flared briefly before he spoke. "How soon can we get you in to see a doctor?"

"A doctor?" she quizzed. "Why?" Sure, she'd been overprotective of James and reluctant about telling her parents the truth, but there wasn't any need for her to see a physician.

"If you're pregnant—"

"Oh, that," she said, relieved. "Taylor recommended that I buy one of those home pregnancy tests at the drugstore, which I did this afternoon. Only I decided I could deal with not knowing better than I could handle knowing. Does that sound crazy?"

Cody chuckled. "No. But do you mind satisfying my curiosity? I, for one, am anxious to know if I'm going to become a father or not."

"You definitely are," she said, loving the way Cody's face brightened at her words. "The only question is whether or not it's going to be sometime within the next nine months."

Cody's arms were around her, his eyes filled with a tenderness that caused her knees to grow weak. "The test takes about twenty minutes," she whispered, sliding her hands up the front of his shirt and leaning into his strength.

"Twenty minutes," Cody repeated.

She moistened her lips and thrilled when her husband's narrowed gaze followed the seductive movement of her tongue. His hands fit over the rounded curve of her buttocks, bringing her more forcefully into contact with the hardening bulge in his pants.

"Are you suggesting what I think you're suggesting?"

Christy nodded.

"But if you are pregnant, will it hurt the baby?" His voice was hoarse, and a dark flame seemed to leap to life from the back of his eyes.

"Not according to Taylor."

"You're sure?"

"Positive. Besides, it will do this baby's mother a whole world of good."

* * *

Christy lay contentedly in his arms, her long, sleek body nestled intimately with his. If they spent the next ten years exactly like this, Cody wouldn't have a single complaint. Dear sweet heaven, he loved his woman. He loved everything about her.

"Are you disappointed?" she asked softly, rolling over so she could look at him when he answered.

He kissed her, his mouth clinging to hers, his hands caressing her. "You've got to be kidding."

They'd been on fire for each other from the moment he'd arrived. Their hands had trembled as they'd hurriedly undressed each other, their mouths eager, filled with promises and pleas.

Christy had been impatient, needing him to hurry, urging him with her hands and her mouth to possess her in ways that made it impossible to deny.

Cody was just as impatient, but he was concerned, not wanting to do anything that would put her or their baby at risk. He'd intended to go slowly, to exercise willful restraint.

Well, at least he'd tried.

But Christy had started writhing mindlessly beneath him, urging him with sighs and whimpers and unspoken demands until Cody had been completely lost in his need for her. They'd made love with a savage tenderness that left them both breathless and satisfied in its aftermath. Together they'd scaled the heights of the heavens, and then returned, lost in a universe that was solely their own.

Raising herself on one elbow, Christy smiled dreamily down on him and lovingly traced her fingers over the hard angles of his face as though memorizing each feature. To Cody's way of thinking, it was an unnecessary exercise. He never planned to be away from her again.

"I wasn't talking about the lovemaking," she said, lightly brushing her mouth over his. "I was referring to the pregnancy test."

His arm curved around her trim waist. "No. When the time's right, we'll start our family and not because we were in too much of a hurry to—"

"May I remind you how much of a hurry we were in a few minutes ago?"

"No, you may not." He gripped her waist with both hands and rolled her onto her back with one swift, effortless movement. Her eyes smiled up at him, then widened briefly at the evidence of his desire.

It was amazing how these things happened, he mused later. He wasn't in the least bit of a rush the second time they made love, but then again he was in too much of one to worry about anything but loving her properly.

"I think it might be a good idea if I went over to my parents' house alone," Christy announced. Before Cody could argue with her she flattened her hands on his chest and looked up at him beseechingly. "You don't know my father the way I do."

"I won't hear of it, Christy," he answered in a voice that brooked little discussion. "We're in this together."

"But..."

"You phoned James?"

"You know I did. He'll arrive at my parents' house within the hour." James had sounded surprised to hear from her, and even more perplexed when she explained she needed to speak with him urgently. He'd offered to come to her apartment immediately, but when she'd suggested they meet at her family home in an hour, he'd agreed somewhat reluctantly.

"How did Rich find out we're telling your parents?" Cody wanted to know, frowning.

Her scoundrel of a brother had been visiting their parents when Christy had phoned. There must have been something in her voice that relayed her intent, because Rich had made it clear he intended to stay around for the fireworks display. The comment, however innocent, reminded Christy that the coming scene was sure to evoke a good deal of emotion. Personally Christy wished Cody would wait for the worst to pass before he presented himself as their latest son-in-law.

"Don't even think of arguing with me," he said, eyeing her sternly. "We're doing this together."

"All right," she said, holding in a sigh so long that her chest ached. "The way I figure it, we'll have forty-five minutes to explain everything to my parents before James arrives."

"Good." Cody nodded.

"Are you ready?" she asked, and her voice trembled despite every effort to maintain an optimistic facade. Her heart felt frozen with trepidation, her nerves shot. Although she'd wanted Cody to let her handle this on her own, she was eternally grateful he'd chosen to go with her.

They spoke infrequently on the drive over to her parents' home. When they did, it was to murmur words of encouragement to each other, or reinforce the fact they were deeply in love and committed.

When they pulled into the driveway, another car came in after them. "Oh, no," Christy breathed.

"What's wrong?"

"It's James." Christy climbed out of the car, not waiting for Cody. She turned to face her fiancé. "You're early," she commented, struggling to keep the censure out of her voice.

"I called your parents, and they suggested I come now." James's gaze narrowed as Cody came to stand behind her and rested his hand on her shoulder.

It was clear James took offense to the familiar way Cody touched her. His eyes went cold as he demanded, "Who is this?"

Chapter Fourteen

Christy felt Cody's hand involuntarily tighten. The two men glared at each other like hostile dogs who'd inadvertently strayed across each other's territory. It wasn't a complimentary way in which to think of Cody and James, but the analogy seemed fitting.

"James, this is Cody Franklin," she said, hating the unexpected way her voice pitched.

"So the gang's all here," Rich hailed, coming out the front door, ready to greet the two men like long-lost relatives. "I suppose you're wondering why I've called this meeting." He paused and laughed, obviously in a jolly mood.

Christy glared at him, wondering at his game.

"Do you mind waiting a few minutes?" Rich asked. "Jason and Paul are on their way."

"As a matter of fact, I do mind," Christy snapped. She gripped Rich hard by the elbow and marched him back into the house. "Kindly introduce Cody to Mom and Dad," she instructed.

Rich's mouth sagged open. "Me? No way, little sister. I happen to value my neck."

"I'll take care of everything," Cody said, slapping Rich across the back. "You have nothing to fear but fear itself."

"James," Christy said reproachfully, turning to face the attorney, "it would have helped matters if you'd come when I suggested, but since you're here now, we'll settle this in the kitchen."

She walked into the house and passed her mother, who was staring at her with openmouthed wonder.

"We'll talk in the kitchen," Christy reminded James when he hesitated in front of Elizabeth Manning and shrugged.

"Christy?" her father called, sounding more than a little baffled. "What's going on here?"

"I'll explain everything in a few minutes, but first I have to clear up a matter with James."

"Actually, I'll be more than happy to explain things," Cody said, stepping forward. He offered Eric Manning his hand, and the two exchanged a brief handshake as Cody introduced himself.

"Exactly what's going on?" James wanted to know as they entered the kitchen.

Christy stopped at the huge round oak table. She pulled out a chair and sat down, then gestured for James to do the same.

He complied, but with some hesitation. "You never answered my question. Who is that man?"

"Cody Franklin."

"That doesn't explain much."

"No, it doesn't," she agreed readily. Releasing a slow sigh, she wondered where she should even begin. What had seemed so simple a few weeks earlier was complicated to the extreme now. "He's from Montana."

"Ah, that explains the cowboy hat."

"We met when I went to spend time with Taylor. Cody's the new sheriff of Custer County."

James nodded, urging her to go on. She'd just explained the easy part; everything else that remained was increasingly difficult.

Unable to remain sitting, Christy surged to her feet and rubbed her palms together while she organized her thoughts. "Sometimes, not often I think, but sometimes when two strangers meet something happens...something special." She paused and looked at James, hoping, praying she'd see a glimmer of understanding. She didn't.

"You're talking fairy tales," he said, and laughed lightly as though she'd made a poor joke and he found it difficult to find the humor. "Are you going to break into song next?"

Christy ignored the question. "A special magic, a chemistry that flows between the two. There was magic when Taylor met Russ. They both resisted it, fought against it."

"Yes, yes," James interrupted, "but what have your sister and her husband got to do with anything?"

"Cody and I experienced that same...chemistry," she announced, astonished this genius attorney could be so obtuse. "Neither of us was looking to fall in love."

"You didn't," James announced flatly, dismissing her claim.

"But I did," she countered just as smoothly.

"You couldn't be in love with Franklin. It isn't possible when you're already in love with me."

"James, please, let me explain something—"

He interrupted with an upraised hand. "Christy, darling, what you experienced for this man is a simple case of homesickness. It's perfectly understandable, and forgivable. We were only engaged a day or two, and after working so closely together for all those weeks, it only makes sense that you would look to another man for companionship."

"James," she said softly, taking both of his hands in her own, her gaze pleading with him, "that's not the case. I wish it were that simple, but it isn't."

"Nonsense." James hadn't been touted as a brilliant attorney without reason. With infuriating ease, he turned everything she said around to suit his own purposes.

"I love Cody." She said it forcefully enough, she prayed, for James to accept it as truth.

"As I already explained, that isn't possible." He stood and gently placed his hands on her shoulders, his look indulgent. "You love me, remember? Otherwise you wouldn't have agreed to become my wife."

"I agreed to your proposal because it pleased my mother and father," she cried, hating the way he twisted everything around and wanting to set him straight.

"Christy." He said her name softly, as if she were a petulant child. "I'm sure you're mistaken."

"I'm not." She braced her hands against his forearms as she stared directly into his eyes. "I love Cody Franklin so much I married him."

It pained Christy to watch the transformation come over James's features. His face tightened with disbelief. He opened his mouth as if to argue, certain she was playing some heartless joke on him.

"It's true," she said before he could question her.

Intense anger flickered in his eyes. He jerked his arms free from her and dropped them to his sides.

"When?"

"Does it matter when?"

"No, I guess not." His eyes drifted shut briefly, profoundly. The simple action said more than any words he could have spoken.

She took a moment to open the clasp of her purse and reach for the diamond ring he'd given her. When she handed it back to him, James stared at the velvet box as if he'd never seen it before. "Keep it."

"No, I couldn't."

He removed it from her hand and turned away long enough to stuff it into his coat pocket. When he looked to her again, he was able to mask the pain, but she knew him well enough to realize she'd shocked and hurt him deeply. Causing him such intense pain was the most difficult thing she'd ever have to do. James didn't deserve to be treated this way.

"I fully intended to tell you the minute I arrived home from Montana," she said in her own defense, the words coming so fast they nearly blended together.

"The engagement party," he supplied for her. "You tried to say something to me then, didn't you?" He didn't wait for her to answer. "I sensed something was wrong and trapped you into setting a wedding date." He scowled, the action drawing his thick brows together in the center of his forehead. "On a subconscious level I ignored the obvious, immersed myself in my work, hoping whatever had happened with you would pass. I know I made it difficult to talk to me. But am I that unreasonable that you couldn't have told me the truth. Am I that unreasonable?''

"That wasn't it." It was important to Christy that she correct that impression. "I didn't feel I could. You were so heavily involved in the Mulligan case and I didn't want to—''

"I'm still involved."

"I know. But the worst of it's over, and I couldn't go on pretending any longer. I'm sorry, James, sorrier than you'll ever realize.''

He snickered softly, but didn't openly contradict her.

"I'm terribly fond of you and I'd give anything to—''

"Fond." He spit out the word as if it were an obscenity.

His vehemence was a shock. James wasn't a passionate man. Rarely had Christy seen him reveal any emotion, in or out of a courtroom.

Once more she tried to explain. "I can't and don't expect you to understand how difficult this was for me. That would be asking too much of you." She knew she sounded shaken, but she couldn't seem to help that. "If there were any possible way I could have done this without hurting you, I would have.''

He didn't respond.

"You're a wonderful man, James, and someday a woman will come into your life—the right woman. And you'll know what I mean.''

"You were the right woman, or so I believed.''

"I'm sorry, terribly sorry.''

He shook his head as if he couldn't quite believe her, even now. His hand was buried in his pocket, and Christy guessed he'd made a tight fist around the diamond.

"I only wish you the best," she whispered.

He breathed deeply once, then nodded, although Christy had the impression he wasn't agreeing with her. She was about to say something more when a thunderous shout of objection came from the direction of the living room.

"Your father?" James asked.

Christy nodded. "Cody must have told him."

James's gaze continued to hold hers. "You'll be all right?"

"Of course."

He seemed to accept that. "Can I kiss you one last time?"

In response she opened her arms to him and nodded, her eyes brimming with unshed tears. James reached for her, his touch light and gentle. He held her close for just a moment, then pressed his mouth to hers in a tender exchange.

He broke away, and his finger touched her cheek, his eyes dark and clouded. "Be happy, Christy."

"I will."

With that he turned and walked out of the kitchen. Christy watched him move down the walkway from the kitchen window. A ragged sigh rumbled through her chest as he climbed inside his car. For what seemed an eternity, James sat in the driver's seat with his hands gripping the steering wheel as he stared straight ahead.

Christy couldn't delay the confrontation with her family any longer. Squaring her shoulders, she moved into the living room to find her brothers, Paul, Jason and Rich, perched atop bar stools as though viewing a stage performance.

"Christy," her mother sobbed, dabbing a tissue under her nose, "tell us it isn't true."

She moved next to Cody and sat on the arm of the chintz-covered chair. He tucked his arm around her waist. "Cody and I were married last week."

"Married!" Her father stormed to his feet as if she'd dared to desecrate the Constitution of the United States.

Confused, Christy's gaze clashed with Cody's.

"I hadn't gotten around to telling them that part yet," he explained.

"Married," her mother repeated. "It can't be true. Christy would never do anything so... We have a wedding to plan. You couldn't possibly have gone off and gotten married without telling your own mother and father. It isn't like you to do something so underhanded."

"I thought they knew," she whispered, bewildered. "I heard Dad give a shout, and I thought...I assumed."

"All I said," Cody explained, "was that you wanted a little privacy with James so that you could return his engagement ring."

"Oh." She swallowed tightly and closed her eyes in an effort to regain her composure. "Well, Mom and Dad," she said brightly, looking at them once more, "I see you've met your new son-in-law."

"Welcome to the family," Paul said, holding up an aluminum soft drink can in tribute. "From what Rich said, you're a friend of Russ's."

Cody nodded.

"But you couldn't possible be married," her mother whimpered, looking at Eric as though he would be the one to explain everything.

"Trust me, Mom, we're married."

"They're married," Rich said, saluting them with his own can of soda. "I should know. I was there for the wedding night."

"Here, here," Jason cried, wearing the ever-present baseball cap and looking aghast. "On their wedding night? Tell all, brother dearest."

"I don't find any of this the least bit humorous or in good taste," Eric roared. "Your sister's turned down the best man in three states for some county lawman. It was bad enough that Taylor had to marry a rancher, but Christy, too? Never."

"Dad," Christy reminded him softly, "the deed is done."

"But, Christy," Elizabeth wailed, "I bought the material for the bridesmaids' dresses and we've put a deposit down on the hall for the reception, and..."

"I didn't mean to cheat you out of a wedding, Mom. I really didn't."

"What will we say to our friends?" Her mother appeared to be in a state of shock. She'd gone deathly pale, and her shoulders made several jerky movements as she tried to gain control of her emotions.

"If you're worried about what to tell your friends," Paul said, sounding knowledgeable and experienced in these matters, "I'd suggest the truth."

"Stay out of this," Eric barked, dismissing his eldest son with a hard shake of his hand. "We're in one hell of a mess here."

"How's that?" Cody asked.

"Christy's married to you is why," Eric informed him none too gently. "My daughter doesn't belong in the country. She was born and raised in the city. It's bad enough that Taylor's living out in the tules. I won't allow Christy to be out there slopping hogs or whatever else it is you do in that backwoods community.''

"Dad!" Christy was outraged. "Cougar Point isn't any backwoods community. Besides, we won't be living there."

"You're moving to Washington State?" Elizabeth asked Cody, her eyes wide and hopeful.

"Sorry, no."

Her mother sagged against the back of the sofa and reached for a fresh tissue. She wadded it up and pressed it over her eyes as if to block out this horrible scene.

"Cody's the sheriff," Christy explained, wanting to impress both of her parents with the fact he was a responsible citizen. "We'll be living in Miles City once he's installed."

"A sheriff should impress them," Jason said under his breath, speaking to his two brothers.

"I think they prefer an attorney over a sheriff," Rich concluded when neither parent gave any indication of speaking.

"I recognize that this is all rather abrupt," Cody said in a reasonable tone of voice. "I can't blame you for being shocked. I don't even blame you for being concerned. You wouldn't have raised a daughter as wonderful as Christy if you weren't the kind of people you are."

"That's good," Paul whispered to Jason. "He's going to win them over with flattery."

"Will you three kindly shut up," Eric barked, infuriated with his sons and not bothering to disguise it.

"Dad, please try to understand," Christy tried once more. "I fell in love with Cody."

"Falling in love is one thing, but marrying him on the sly is another."

"While she was engaged to James, I might add." Rich apparently didn't know when to keep his mouth closed. Both Eric and Cody sent daggers his way. Guarding his face with his hands, Rich pretended to ward off their unexpected attack.

"I can only say I love you both," Christy said softly. "I'd never do anything intentional to hurt you. In fact, most of my life I've done everything I can to please you, right down to becoming engaged to James."

"I can't believe I'm hearing this," Eric said to his wife. "We raised her as best we knew how, and now this."

"Darling, we thought you loved James," her mother pleaded.

"I thought I did, too, until I met Cody." Her hand clasped Cody's, and she smiled down on him. "I know I made mistakes, lots of them."

"*We* made mistakes," Cody corrected, his gaze holding hers.

"No one's making up a list," her father mumbled, "but if I were—"

"Nothing on this green earth will ever convince me I made a mistake marrying Cody." It was apparent her father wasn't going to willingly accept what they'd done. As Christy suspected, her family would need a little time to come to terms with the fact she was married and would be leaving the Seattle area.

"I gave my week's notice when I returned from vacation," Christy explained. It had been one of the low points of her life, telling Marcia she was going to stop working in order to prepare for her wedding. The lie had all but choked her.

"You're leaving your job?"

"She couldn't very well continue working with James," Eric explained to his wife. "And from the sounds of it, she intends to live in Montana."

"Poor James," Elizabeth said on the tail end of a regret-filled sigh. "He would have made such a good husband."

"I'll make Christy a good husband, too," Cody promised. "I love your daughter."

An awkward silence followed Cody's words. "My daughter doesn't belong in Montana, and she certainly deserves a decent wedding with her family surrounding her. Christy's not the type of girl a man takes to a justice of the peace."

"We were married by a minister." Christy knew even before she explained that there was little she could say that would appease her father. He was master of his house and wasn't accustomed to having his authority challenged. Not even by a sheriff.

"It might be best if we give your parents some time to think everything through," Cody suggested.

Christy agreed, but leaving her family home was one of the most difficult tasks of her life.

Paul, Jason and Rich followed them outside.

"They'll come around," Paul said to Cody as they exchanged handshakes. Paul was tall and silver-blond, the only one in the family who'd inherited the striking coloring.

"Just give 'em a year or three," Rich said with less than diplomatic cheer. "Grandkids will be sure to win them over. There will be children, won't there?" He was eyeing Christy as if a good stare in the eye would tell him if she was in the family way.

"Don't worry about a thing," Jason said, looping his arm over Cody's broad shoulders. "Mom and Dad will accept the fact you're married before you know it."

"They've got two days," Cody announced darkly.

"Two days?" Christy echoed, a little stunned, although she shouldn't have been. Cody's life was in Miles City, and he'd recently taken three days of his vacation to spend time with her. He couldn't afford to take off any more time, not during this important period of transition.

"Is that too soon for you?" he asked, his eyes revealing his concern. "I figured that would give us enough time to get your things packed up and shipped."

She nodded, slipping her arms around his waist and hugging him close. Her life was linked to Cody's now, and there was no turning back.

The seat assignment had already been called, but Christy delayed boarding, glancing around the terminal building, certain if she stayed there long enough her parents would rush in and throw their arms around her, telling her how much they loved her and how they wished her and Cody well.

Only they hadn't come, and it was all too obvious they had no intention of coming to see her and Cody off.

"Honey," Cody said patiently, gently, gripping her around the waist. "They aren't coming."

"I know, but I'd hoped. I . . . thought they'd at least want to say goodbye."

Christy hadn't heard from them in the two hectic days they'd spent packing up her apartment. She'd tried not to let it affect her, but she'd always been close to her parents, and having them shun her this way hurt more than anything they could have said.

"Give them time," Cody said, and it seemed as if her pain belonged to him, too.

Christy offered him a brave smile and nodded.

Their flight number was called once more, and glancing over her shoulder, Christy realized there was nothing left for them to do but board the plane that would lead her away from the only home she'd ever known to one she'd never seen.

"You're not sorry, are you?" Cody asked once they were seated and were about to take off.

"Never." Beyond a doubt Christy knew she was meant to be with Cody. She would have preferred to have her parents' blessing. But if she had to do without it, then she would learn to accept that.

Cody was her love. Cody was her life. The time had come to set the old aside and start with the new.

Since Paul, Jason and Rich all worked days and wouldn't be able to come to the airport in midday to say their goodbyes, the three had taken Christy and Cody to dinner together the night before.

Everyone had made an effort to have a good time, and they had.

Only it felt as if something vital was missing. No one said anything. No one had to.

Eric and Elizabeth Manning were what was missing. Their love. Their blessing. Their approval.

Christy had no idea how long it would take.

"Oh, Cody," Christy whispered, stepping back to examine her husband in full dress uniform. She pressed her hands over her lips and shook her head in awe. "You look . . . beautiful."

They'd been in Montana a week. In that time they'd moved into their first home, unpacked their belongings and gone about making a place for themselves in the community.

"What time will Russ and Taylor be here?"

"Oh," she said, still a little awed by how incredibly handsome her husband looked. "I forgot to tell you Taylor phoned. They're going to meet us at the courthouse for the installation."

"Good." He straightened the sleeves of his crisp uniform jacket. "Well, I'm ready."

"I'm not," Christy reminded him. "In case you haven't noticed, I'm not dressed yet."

Cody wiggled his eyebrows suggestively. "All the better to ravish you, my dear."

Christy giggled. "I do believe you've ravished me in every room of this house, Sheriff Franklin. More than once."

"There's time—"

"There most certainly is not," she claimed, scooting past him. She wasn't quick enough, and with little effort, Cody pinned her to the wall. His eyes held hers as the lower half of his body moved suggestively over her.

"Cody," she cautioned. "We...can't. Either you'll be late for your own installation, or your wife will arrive looking like a wicked witch."

Cody hesitated. "You're a tempting morsel."

She entwined her arms around his neck and kissed him soundly, outlining the curve of his mouth with her tongue, seducing him with her hands and her body until he sagged weakly against her.

"Now, husband dearest, you have a decision to make. Is it law and order or pagan sacrifice?"

"Ah..." he hesitated. She slowly rotated her hips against him. He mumbled a curse, and with some effort managed to pull himself away from her. "Get dressed before you give me any other ideas."

"Aye, aye, sir." Mockingly she saluted him.

A half hour later they entered the courthouse. Judge Carter would be doing the honors, and the room was filled to capacity. Christy was escorted to the front row of reserved seats. Many of the good citizens from Cougar Point filled the audience.

The ceremony was just about to begin when Taylor, carrying Eric, and Russ slipped into the chairs to her right. That left two empty seats on her left. Christy was so busy greeting her sister that she didn't notice the vacant chairs were filled. She turned to smile and introduce herself to her seatmates, and to her astonishment discovered her parents.

"Mom. Dad," she cried softly. Without warning, tears flooded her eyes. She smeared them across her face and looked at Cody, who was standing at the podium with Judge Carter. Their gazes met, and when she nodded toward her family, Cody's face brightened.

"Are you willing to forgive your father for being a stubborn old cuss?" Eric asked.

Christy nodded, shaken by the enormity of her relief. She hugged him close and then her mother, who was as teary-eyed as Christy.

When the ceremony was over, Cody joined them. Christy's husband and father faced each other. Eric Manning offered his hand first, and the two exchanged a hearty shake.

Judge Carter came forward and introduced himself, and soon they were all talking at once.

A small reception followed, and Cody gripped Christy's hand as he led the way.

"Thank you," she whispered.

He looked somewhat taken back. "Honey, as much as I'd like to take credit for bringing your parents out, I can't."

"Not that," she said, smiling up at him from the very depth of her soul. "Thank you for loving me."

"That," he said softly, "was the easiest, most natural thing I've ever done."

"Eric Manning," Christy could hear her father say over the din of raised voices. "I'm the sheriff's father-in-law. We're right proud of the boy. Glad to have him in the family."

"Not as glad as he is to be part of it," Cody murmured, smiling at his wife.

* * * * *

WRITTEN IN THE STARS

**Star-crossed lovers?
Or a match made in heaven?**

Why are some heroes strong and silent . . . and others charming and cheerful? The answer is WRITTEN IN THE STARS! Coming each month in 1991, Silhouette Romance presents you with a special love story written by one of your favorite authors—highlighting the hero's astrological sign! From January's sensible Capricorn to December's disarming Sagittarius, you'll meet a dozen dazzling heroes.

Sexy, serious Justin Starbuck wasn't about to be tempted by his aunt's lovely hired companion, but Philadelphia Jones thought his love life needed her helping hand! What happens when this cool, conservative Capricorn meets his match in a sweet, spirited blonde like Philadelphia?

The answer leads to THE UNDOING OF JUSTIN STARBUCK by Marie Ferrarella, available in January at your favorite retail outlet, or order your copy by sending your name, address, zip or postal code, along with a check or money order for $2.25 (please do not send cash), plus 75¢ postage and handling, payable to Silhouette Reader Service to:

In the U.S.
3010 Walden Ave.
P.O. Box 1396
Buffalo, NY 14269-1396

In Canada
P.O. Box 609
Fort Erie, Ontario
L2A 5X3

Please specify book title with your order. Canadian residents add applicable federal and provincial taxes.

Silhouette Books

JANSTAR

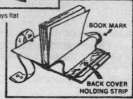

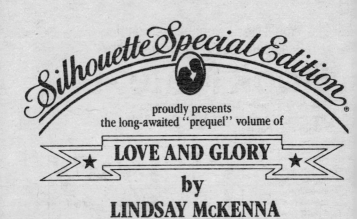

Silhouette Special Edition

proudly presents
the long-awaited "prequel" volume of

LOVE AND GLORY ★

by
LINDSAY McKENNA

Dawn of Valor

In the summer of '89, Silhouette Special Edition premiered three novels celebrating America's men and women in uniform: LOVE AND GLORY, by bestselling author Lindsay McKenna. Featured were the proud Trayherns, a military family as bold and patriotic as the American flag—three siblings valiantly battling the threat of dishonor, determined to triumph...in love and glory.

Now, discover the roots of the Trayhern brand of courage, as parents Chase and Rachel relive their earliest heartstopping experiences of survival and indomitable love, in

Dawn of Valor, Silhouette Special Edition #649.

This February, experience the thrill of LOVE AND GLORY—from the very beginning!

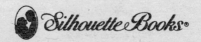

Silhouette Books